# PART-TIME LOVER

LAUREN BLAKELY

# COPYRIGHT

# ALSO BY LAUREN BLAKELY

**Big Rock Series**

*Big Rock*

*Mister O*

*Well Hung*

*Full Package*

*Joy Ride*

*Hard Wood*

**One Love Series dual-POV Standalones**

*The Sexy One*

*The Only One*

*The Hot One*

**Sports Romances**

*Most Valuable Playboy*

*Most Likely to Score*

**Standalones**

*The Knocked Up Plan*

*The Start of Us*

*Every Second With You*


**The Seductive Nights Series**

*First Night* (Julia and Clay, prequel novella)

*Night After Night* (Julia and Clay, book one)

*After This Night* (Julia and Clay, book two)

*One More Night* (Julia and Clay, book three)

*A Wildly Seductive Night* (Julia and Clay novella, book 3.5)


**The Joy Delivered Duet**

*Nights With Him* (A standalone novel about Michelle and Jack)

*Forbidden Nights* (A standalone novel about Nate and Casey)


**The Sinful Nights Series**

*Sweet Sinful Nights*

*Sinful Desire*

*Sinful Longing*

*Sinful Love*


**The Fighting Fire Series**

*Burn For Me* (Smith and Jamie)

*Melt for Him* (Megan and Becker)

*Consumed By You* (Travis and Cara)

**The Jewel Series**

A two-book sexy contemporary romance series

*The Sapphire Affair*

*The Sapphire Heist*

## ABOUT PART-TIME LOVER

**I'll say this about Christian — he made one hell of a first impression.** When I first saw the strapping man, he was doing handstands naked on a dock along the canal. His crown jewels were far more entertaining than anything else I'd seen on the boat tour, so I did what any curious woman would do — I took his photo. I might have looked at the shot a few dozen times. Little did I know I'd meet him again, a year later, at a secret garden bar in the heart of the city, where I'd learn that his mind and his mouth were even more captivating. But given the way my heart had been trampled, I wanted only a simple deal — No strings. No expectations.

**Our arrangement worked well enough until the day I needed a lot more from him...**

\*\*\*

Let me just say, this whole part-time lover thing was her idea. I'd have gone all-in from the start, but hey, when a gorgeous, brilliant woman invites you into her bed, and only her bed...well, I said yes.

But then, one hysterical phone call from my brother later, begging me to find myself a wife so grandfather's business stays in the family, and I need a promotion with Elise. **Turns out a full-time husband suits her needs too,** and a temporary marriage of convenience ought to do the trick, until we can simply untie the knot...

*As long as no one finds out...*
   *As long as no one gets hurt...*
   *As long as no one falls in love...*

**But our ending was one I never saw coming.**

## 1

## ELISE

*A year ago*

Something about the last night in a foreign city makes you want to do crazy things. You want to drink it all in and taste every single dish on the menu. After all, tomorrow you'll be gone.

Left with only memories.

The last night is the last stop on the merry-go-round of memory-making.

The last afternoon is too, and as the sun careens mercilessly toward the horizon, it's a reminder that I need to jam everything in.

"Do you feel like going a little bit wild?" I ask Veronica.

She wiggles her eyebrows. "If you mean day drinking, we've already done that."

I wag my finger as we stroll down the middle of a

cobbled street. "One glass of wine at lunch does not constitute day drinking."

"No? That seems the very definition."

I link an arm through hers. "One glass is simply a beverage at lunch. The meter doesn't start on day drinking until you hit two glasses, silly goose."

"How good to know the scale for lushness," she says drily as she stops to stare at a handbag in the Prada store window.

I give her a few seconds to worship at the altar of designer goods. "In any case, I was thinking we ought to do something we've never done before."

She snaps her gaze from the far-too-expensive leather item she'll never buy and presses a hand demurely to her chest, batting her hazel eyes innocently. "I'm not that kind of girl."

I laugh. "As if."

"I know. You like your sausage too much."

"As do you. You're practically a butcher," I say as we sidestep a pair of strapping, chiseled blond men, who look like twin models for Scandinavian Design's "Catalog of Men—Denmark." Their blue eyes linger on both of us, and one smiles and offers a confident, "Hello."

"Hello to you too," I say with a grin.

They continue in their direction and we head in ours. "Should we wander down the streets and say hello to random hot men?" Veronica offers.

"I don't think that's a bad idea, but no, that's not my notion of wild."

This urge to have one wild night is in complete

contrast to the purpose of the three-days-in-Copenhagen getaway Veronica insisted I needed.

*It's been a year since . . .*

I shake away the dark thought.

Anniversaries of horrible days require trips. And day drinking. And refocusing on things that you control.

"If I want to explore the travel sector more at work, I need to know even more about this city, so I can advertise it better. What if we take one of those buffet boat tours?"

She laughs. "What's a buffet boat tour?"

"A buffet of landmarks. All-your-eyes-can-eat." As we near the wide square at the end of the block, I point to the red booth advertising canal tours. I play my ace. "It's like a crash course in Copenhagen, and we'll make sure we haven't missed a single thing. It'll help me win new business. You know I need to focus on work."

She smiles in understanding. "Anything for you when you prey on my sympathies." She marches up to the fire-engine-red booth and purchases two tickets for the next tour, then we head down the concrete steps to the boat.

The blond guide with shoulder-length hair flashes a bright smile as we step onboard, his name tag glinting in the afternoon sun. "Good afternoon, ladies."

"Lars, she's no lady." Veronica points to me and winks.

"Ladies or not, you're both welcome on my ship as long as you promise to enjoy the sights."

"We will. Also, you're handsome, Lars." Veronica is a shameless flirt.

"Thank you very much, and I'll enjoy the sights as well." It seems Lars is a flirt too. His blue-eyed gaze lingers on my friend with the hourglass figure and pretty eyes as we take our seats.

We wait for the boat to fill, but only a handful of others join us. An older couple sports cameras around their necks and matching *I Heart Copenhagen* backpacks. There is also a gaggle of twenty-something women wearing college sweatshirts and some Japanese tourists.

I lean back in the cushioned seat, dropping my sunglasses to shield my eyes as the boat peels away from the dock. As we slide over the placid water, Lars regales us with tales of royal families and scandals, pointing out the city's sights. I lean closer to Veronica and whisper, "Will you pick up where you left off with the handsome boat captain?"

Lars suffers from an affliction common to many men in Denmark. He's a cut above average in the looks department. Let the record reflect, the Danes make the best-looking men.

"Of course. I'm going to talk to him when the tour ends."

"Excellent. I love your planning skills."

The boat slides under another bridge then motors through a more residential area, passing homes on the water and private docks every few feet. My eyes hungrily eat up the view. My current hometown of Paris is my love, but I could get used to weekends in Copenhagen. It's a delightful mix of old and new, like a Swiss alpine town mated with a futuristic sky-rise city.

As I gaze at the sun-soaked homes, I imagine lazy

afternoons drinking strong coffee on the deck, reading delicious tales under the rays. That seems like a recipe for happiness for the rest of my days.

I want to feel that way. *Happy.* It's been so damn elusive lately, and for a fleeting moment, it feels as if I grasp it again, so I'm no longer teetering on the edge of grief and shame.

But that's why I'm here, to move past that terrible duet.

I try valiantly to simply enjoy everything in front of me: the buildings, the water, the view.

As we round the bend in the canal, I blink *at* the view.

Holy hell, the unexpected view.

Nearby is a private dock.

On that dock is a man.

He's performing a downward-facing dog, and his rear is facing us.

What a spectacular ass.

It's not covered in sweatpants or basketball shorts.

It's au naturel, as finely sculpted as the statue of David.

He's a dog all right.

I sit up.

I practically stand. I lean on the edge of the boat, agog. I won't even pretend I'm not looking. I'm ogling.

The Japanese friends whisper and point. The couple shifts closer to get a better look. The college girls titter and laugh.

We slide along on the calm water, and now we're fifty feet away from a sight way better than the Little

Mermaid statue, more magnificent than the royal palace.

He bends forward, pressing his palms into the wood, lifting his legs, and flipping them upside down.

Full. Frontal. Birthday suit.

He's a tall drink of man, and I'm so very thirsty.

"Look," I whisper to Veronica, though of course she's already engaged in the fine art of gawking. "Did you know the Mad Naked Handstander of Copenhagen was on the tour?"

She sighs contentedly. "I am so glad you forced me to go to the buffet." She parks her chin in her hands, watching the tall upside-down creature.

"My favorite part of the buffet is dessert," I say, as my eyes gobble him up.

This man wears nudity well, even in this unusual position.

"I enjoyed the rubies and emeralds in Rosenborg Castle, but I like these crown jewels even better," I say.

And hey, perhaps I'm perving, but I'm an equal-opportunity spectator at this private dock show. I don't merely peer at the centerpiece of his physique, resting majestically against the grooves of his abs. My eyes take a most happy stroll up and down his carved body, from the planes of his stomach, to his strong thighs, to his arms ripped with muscles. His face is hard to read at 180 degrees, but I see the shape of his cheekbones, carved by angels.

Then, he moves. He walks on his hands. Back and forth.

Like he's performing.

Showing off his most unique skill set.

I chuckle louder.

Then louder still when he holds himself up on one hand only, waving to us.

"What a show-off," Veronica says.

Lars clears his throat. "And sometimes, we see the unexpected sights of Copenhagen."

I do what any curious onlooker might do. I grab my phone and snap.

*Snap.*

*Snap.*

The man stands, takes a bow, and waves.

My chest heats up. The temperature in me flirts with mercury levels. He's a stunner. My God, he's like Skarsgård, from this distance.

And because I believe in speaking my mind, I cup my hand over my mouth and shout, "Bravo. All of it."

He doffs an imaginary top hat and takes a bow. "My pleasure." His voice booms across the water, his accent a British one.

Sparks unexpectedly race down my chest. That accent is delicious. "Oh no. The pleasure is truly all mine."

His lips curve up in a smile. A wickedly handsome one. "Then meet me tonight at Jane!"

Veronica nudges me. "That's a club. Say yes. Say it now." Her voice is marked with urgency as we glide away from the dock.

"You're insane," I whisper.

"This is the wild thing to do. Not a boat ride."

Is she crazy?

As the boat motors on, the idea seems both intoxicating and dangerous. Stupid, maybe too. For a second,

I imagine asking Lars to stop the boat. Skarsgård would jump in the water and dolphin his way over to me, parking his hands on the edge of the boat and flashing a gleaming smile, his hair wet, his face covered in droplets of water.

Oh hell, I want to say yes to the naked man.

He barks at me once again, shouting a street name that starts with a *K*, since every word here has a *K* in it, and ends with something like haven. "I'll be there at seven."

I swallow. Is he mad? Am I? Or am I doing what I've told myself I should do for some time now? *Seize the day.*

I cup my hand over the side of my mouth and call out, "Perhaps I'll see you at seven."

Once one of the most beautiful views ever fades from sight, Veronica arches a well-groomed eyebrow. "You're going, right?"

A prickle of nerves skates down my spine. "I am?"

"Did I detect a question mark?"

"Don't you think it's dangerous to have drinks with a man you don't know?"

Shaking her head, she rises, flicks her chestnut-brown hair off her shoulders, and strides purposefully to the front of the boat. Once Lars finishes a tale about the Danish navy and their warships, he lowers his shades, drops his mic, and cocks his head to the side.

Veronica says something to him I can't hear.

But his eyes tell me everything. He's said more than "perhaps."

As she saunters back to me, a determined look in

her eyes, she's daring me to go. She's chosen her own adventure for tonight.

Flopping down in the seat, she declares, "You better get your ass to Jane on whatever street that was." She pokes my shoulder. "You have a date, and so do I."

Why is it that last nights in foreign countries make you do crazy things?

I mean, *think* crazy things.

Clearly, I'm not actually going out with him.

I might have a bath in the marble tub at the hotel, sip a glass of champagne, and lose myself in a new book, the story of a young couple who travel to Rome and get lost and found.

"It's insane."

Veronica grabs my arm, her eyes imploring. "You're not going to his house. That would be insane. You're going to a bar. That's safe."

But is it? Is it safe for my heart?

Once I ask the question, though, I know the answer.

It's only one night. There's nothing safer.

And that's why there's nothing fate can do to stop me. I'm making this choice.

# 2

# CHRISTIAN

Raising my arms to the sky, I give my muscles one final stretch. Really, you can't stretch enough. I plan to be fit and strapping well into my eighties. That's a long way off, but it's always good to prepare for the future.

I turn around, pleased to have knocked out another accomplishment in the ad hoc Welcome to Spring at Fifty-Five Degrees Latitude North club.

Admittedly, it's a bit hammy of us. But it was my turn to flash the canal tourists on behalf of our noble exhibitionist goals, which means my mates will be paying for drinks tomorrow night. Not that I need anyone to pay, but that's the fun of it. I'm well ahead of most of them, since I have friends from university who chicken out when it comes to our little game of "streaking" on the docks for the tour boats.

I never chicken out, no matter the weather. We usually only do it in spring. As many of my fellow club members like to remind me, you'd have to be off your rocker to get naked outside in a Denmark winter. I've been off my rocker a few times. Maybe I like free beer. Or maybe I like surprising other people.

I stroll up the hilly yard toward my house, passing my brother, Erik, who stands close to the porch. "Did you scare them all away? Admit it—they cringed in terror, scary movie–style."

I slash an arm through the air. "Whole boatload of them. Tears, shrieks of horror. Wailing."

He cringes dramatically.

"Toss me a towel, will you? Or do you want to continue to admire your more fit and handsome younger brother?"

Erik scoffs and throws the towel over the porch railing, away from me.

I shrug. "I'll just go inside, and you can check out my arse."

"You can count on me never ever checking out your arse."

I grab the handle on the sliding-glass door and head inside to one of my homes. You can't beat a home on the water. But then, a flat in Paris is hard for me to say no to as well. Good thing I get to have both.

I grab the pair of boxer briefs I left on the couch and tug them on as Erik follows me inside.

"Seriously. How did it go?"

"Exceptionally well. I landed a date tonight."

"Bastard. You're not supposed to get dates when you flash the tourists, and especially not when your beloved brother is only in town with you for a few days." Most of the time Erik's in London, where we were raised.

"Jealous much?" I ask, heading for the fridge and pouring a glass of cold water.

Erik flexes a bicep, then another, posing like he's Mr. Olympia. "I've scored plenty of dates with this fabulous physique. Just none lately."

"That would be because you're married, you tosser."

He flashes a dimpled grin. He's so ridiculously in love with his wife, it's nearly disgusting. He could be the poster child for man-who-falls-arse-over-elbow-for-a-woman. That's something I can't say for all the men in my family.

"I'm like Grandfather, happy as a clam."

I furrow my brow. "How does anyone know clams are happy? Is there a study on clam happiness? We all assume they're rays of sunshine, but how do we know?"

He scratches his chin. "Good question."

"I bet they aren't happy at all. I bet they feel nothing. Is that what happiness should feel like? Nothing?"

He sighs. "Aren't you philosophical today?"

"Maybe. It happens every now and then." I take a drink of the water. "But what can you do? Sometimes deep thoughts stray into my brain, and I can't help it."

"Best to get them out of your head if you have a date tonight."

"Perhaps she likes thinkers," I suggest.

"So, who is she? Did you exchange numbers on the dock? Or did you, I don't know, play charades with your appendages swinging in the breeze?"

"Yes. I can do Morse code with my dick."

"Such a useful skill," he deadpans.

"We did it the old-fashioned way. Picked a spot to meet and a time."

He raises his chin. "And why her? Of all the ladies on all the tours you've ever flashed, you haven't asked one out before. Not that you've told me about anyway."

I let my brain rewind to the petite brunette with the big sunglasses who ogled me unabashedly from the side of the boat. She was pretty, that much I could tell even from fifty feet away.

But pretty alone isn't enough. Pretty is a dime a dozen. I've dated women who aren't pretty, but are witty, clever, and keep me on my toes. I like those traits just as much. Perhaps more. But I'm not opposed to pretty either.

*Obviously.*

"She was bold. She called out *bravo*. She said it louder than anyone ever has."

"So she knows how to read your Morse code."

"She's welcome to read Morse code on me anytime. Come to think of it, she can even treat me like I'm fruit at the market."

Erik laughs. "In some countries, they don't let you touch fruit at the market."

I gesture to my body, from my chest down to my legs. "In the fine country of Christian Land, it's highly encouraged for the bold brunettes to touch the fruit."

"And on that note, I'm off to a meeting," Erik says, clapping me on the back.

The word *meeting* piques my interest. I stand up taller. "Who's it with?"

"Portfolio managers," he says, rubbing his hands together. "We might strike up a partnership. I need to review a few more key details on the way over."

That sends a little thrill down my spine. "Yeah? What sort of deal? What sort of details?"

Erik runs Grandfather's financial firm and has since the old man retired ten years ago. For all intents and purposes, it's his baby now, and he loves it, especially since his wife works with him.

My brother narrows his eyes. "You can't resist, can you?"

"Resist what?"

"You're supposed to be retired. And look at you." He mimes stirring a pot. "Trying to get your hands on the soup."

I scoff. "Please. I'm only curious. I'm not trying to eat your lunch."

"I would never think that. But I told you this would happen, Christian. I told you you'd hate retiring at age twenty-eight. And look—you're proving my point only one year later. Twenty-nine and bored."

"I'm not bored. I'm curious. And asking about your meeting does not prove your point." I swallow and glance at the hardwood floor then back up at him, my tone a bit sheepish. "But could you just humor me and tell me a tiny bit more about it?"

Laughing, he grabs a stool at the island counter, parks himself on it, and proceeds to give me the download on the portfolio managers. My brain whirs, wheels turning and picking up speed as I rattle off ideas here and there, suggestions for what to say, how to negotiate.

Erik grabs his phone and taps out notes, nodding. "Brilliant, brilliant," he mutters.

When he stands, he offers me his hand. "I hate that you're so smart, but I'm glad you let me access that brain of yours."

"What can I say? I have a head for strategy and a body for sin."

He sneers. "I think my breakfast came back up."

Laughing, I show him the door. "I need to go say hi to Mum. Let me know how the meeting goes."

"Let me know how the date goes."

"I'll preempt myself and tell you now—it went perfectly."

"Cocky bastard." He leaves.

A few minutes later, I shower, dress, and head to my mum's flat by the harbor. We watch an episode of our favorite American TV show—the one about regular government employees who happen to possess extraordinary superpowers—then she asks me if I've been behaving at the docks.

"Never."

"You're going to get arrested for public indecency at some point, young man."

"Please. That only happens in America. Who'd arrest me in Europe?"

Laughing, she practically shoves me out the door. "I'm not posting your bail."

"Of course you are. You're the only one who has access to all my accounts."

When I leave, I head to the hip new lounge, Jane, more eager than I expected to be. Funny, how I spent all of thirty seconds with that woman this afternoon. Thirty seconds, fifty feet across the water, with a boatful of others watching on. But even so, I *want* to see her.

Talk to her.

Entertain her.

From her voice, she sounded American, but not entirely. I think she might be French too.

I don't really care where she's from though.

I care where she's going.

Hopefully, home tonight with me.

# 3

# ELISE

Dark jeans, pewter-gray ankle boots that boost me up a critical three inches to a whopping five and a half feet, and a black blouse, the top button undone to show a hint of flesh. Well, I'm not a nun.

I screw up the corner of my lips, peering at myself in the hotel mirror. I'm so . . . dark. "I look like a widow," I mutter.

"No. You look like a trendy, modern woman who likes black," Veronica corrects as she slides chandelier earrings into her ears. She wrenches her gaze back, studying one earlobe. "Why am I wearing these? They might get stuck on a pillow."

"Or a chair cushion. Don't rule out the possibility of rambunctious furniture sex." I wink.

"You're right. Best to wear studs."

She bustles out of the bathroom, grabs her jewelry case from her suitcase, and finds, I presume, the studs she's looking for. Meanwhile, I root around in my bag for another option. Locating a silky purple top, I tug it on. It slides off one shoulder. Just the right amount of sex appeal without being inappropriate.

I hold out my arms wide, giving a half twirl. "How do I look now?"

"Like an eggplant."

I roll my eyes. "You're a witch."

"A very sexy eggplant. Please. It was a compliment."

I eye her getup, which can be described in one word —*clingy*. "And you look positively like a woman who's going to enjoy the fuck out of her last night in town."

She grins widely. "Let's hope I enjoy the fuck out of it." She wiggles her hips. "Also, no need to wait up for me."

"As if I'd wait up for you."

I smooth a hand over my blouse as my stomach flips with nerves. "Am I really doing this?"

"Yes." She slides her foot into a red stiletto. "Aren't you always telling me to enjoy life's pleasures? To take a lover? To savor each day?"

I tap my chin, smirking. "That does sound vaguely like me. But only in theory."

"It's exactly like you," she says adamantly as she slicks on lip gloss. "Now let's put it into practice. You've been talking 'seize the day' ever since you finally came up for air after—"

I wince.

I don't like hearing his name. I don't want her to say his name. Once, not so long ago, his was the only name I ever wanted to hear. At night, in bed—all day long.

Veronica quickly reroutes herself, like a GPS after a wrong turn. "And I love your *carpe diem*-isms. So, let's go *carpe* the hell out of the night. Besides, why is it less crazy for me to see Lars than for you to see . . ." She trails off, waving her hand as if to say you-know-who.

I point to her. "That. Right there. That's why it's less crazy. I don't even know my pseudo-date's name."

"Maybe it's better that way," she says softly, her words laced with meaning.

Maybe she's right. When you've had your heart shredded in a Cuisinart, then your sense of order in the universe sliced off at the knees with a serrated blade, maybe it is best to do things differently.

Tonight will be different. Tonight doesn't have to lead to anything more. Tonight can be a moment in time. A pleasure I take, not just one I talk about.

We leave our room, head down the escalator, and through the brass revolving door that swooshes us onto the street. The doorman hails a taxi, and we slide inside.

Veronica gives the driver two names. "I have no idea which one is closer, but I checked on my GPS, so I think it's—"

"I don't need a GPS. I know exactly where both are. I will take you first," the driver says. A few minutes later, he drops Veronica at a restaurant, and then he shoots me a grin.

"Who needs GPS? I've lived here my whole life. There isn't a sight in this city I can't find." He taps his forehead and smiles confidently at me in the rearview mirror.

A few minutes later, the car jimmies up to the curb, and he smacks a meaty paw on the black leather seat. "See? No GPS, and here you are."

"Brilliant," I say, and press the fare into his palm.

On the street, I glance up at the sign.

It's a little bistro.

"Huh," I mumble, because it looked bigger when I checked it out on Yelp. But if I've learned anything from my decade in advertising, it's that photos can beguile you.

But it's cute enough, and I head inside, my pulse skittering in excitement.

My God, what if he's a serial killer?

*Don't leave with him, then, girl.*

What if he's a lech?

*Walk away.*

What if he's not even here?

*He'll show.*

I do a clean sweep of the bistro and its ten tables and Lilliputian bar. There is no Skarsgård look-alike.

Perhaps he's in the little boys' room.

*Or little lads' room.*

Thinking of his English accent makes me smile, and I grab a seat at the bar and order a glass of white wine. I'm sure he'll be here any minute. You don't ask a woman out while dressed in nothing and then ghost her.

I glance around, then fiddle with a napkin. I need something to do.

Do I stare at my phone as I wait? Or does that make me look too millennial? I don't want to seem like I'm scrolling through my Facebook feed like an addict when he wanders in.

The bartender slides over a glass, and I pay, then engage in small talk with him—the spring weather, how it's been a warm season, and so on.

That kills all of two minutes.

Drumming my fingers on the bar, I straighten my shoulders and sip my wine.

And I wait.

And I wait.

Screw not looking like a phone-obsessed junkie. I have a magazine on my cell phone, and I'm going to read a long, in-depth article on growth in the travel sector. There. I'll be doing business, like I'm not even waiting for him.

I'm keeping myself occupied, and if he shows, fine.

I barely notice the men who stroll into the bistro as I read. Well, I do notice that none look like the man from the dock. I do catalog that none have the impish grin of the handstander.

I'm keenly aware that it's seven thirty-five and my wineglass is empty, and the sector is growing at 11 percent with the biggest opportunity being on the luxury side, and I'm done, I'm done, I'm done.

No one stands me up.

I leave, hail a cab, and return to the hotel where I promptly get acquainted with the way my evening was intended to unfold: a bubble bath, some music, and a novel.

After I've finished soaking, I grab one of those plush hotel bathrobes I never use because I'm not a person who likes bathrobes—since nudity or clothes seem like vastly more reasonable choices—but tonight feels like a bathrobe kind of night.

Bathrobes are for disappointment.

It's easier to drown your temporary sorrow while wearing terry cloth.

Flopping down on the bed, I crack open my book again.

A little while later the door creaks, then it slides open with a loud, demanding groan. Laughter spills into the room. A man with a soft lilt to his English accent says, "I'll make your last night so worth it."

*Worth it.*

Those words resonate with me.

Trysts can make a night worthwhile. Can make a moment sing.

I'm glad Veronica's going to have a fabulous night.

Even if it means my game plan has changed.

They stumble around the corner, and I wave at Veronica and Lars. Her lipstick is smeared. I hold up a hand before she can even breathe a word. "I'll go make myself scarce in the lobby bar."

"You're a saint," Lars says to me with a flirty smile. "A French saint. And she's a French angel."

"I don't think she's an angel, Lars," I say.

"Even better." He buries his face against her neck, smothering her skin in kisses.

"You don't mind?" Veronica's breath catches. "Oh my."

That last comment was not meant for me.

"Enjoy yourself. Seize the night."

"I will," she says breathily. "Did you already seize yours?"

"He didn't show."

She knits her brow. "He didn't?"

"Trust me, I scanned all of Jane for my hand-stander," I say, tugging on panties and leggings under the robe, then dipping into the bathroom to pull on a sweatshirt.

When I pop out, Lars lifts his chin at me. "Did you go to Jane the bistro, or *The Jane*, the hip, trendy lounge bar that's supposed to be popular with French ex-pats down on Kronerghaven?"

I freeze. "Are you kidding me? There are two Janes?"

Lars laughs, as he yanks Veronica impossibly closer. "It's such an easy name to say and to spell. It was good for the tourists. But the newest one is The Jane."

Veronica gasps and jumps up and down. "You know he went to the other Jane. You could still go and find him."

Her excitement is adorable and thoroughly misplaced. I shake my head. "It's eleven thirty. Have fun. Good night."

"*Bonsoir*," Lars says, a dirty sound to his voice that makes it clear he intends to give Veronica a hefty dose of *bonsoir*.

Grabbing my book, my glasses, and my phone, I head to the bar.

I've no interest in drinking though, so I find an empty chair at the edge of the lobby bar and tuck my feet under my legs.

I read till one in the morning.

With no sign of Veronica, I head to the front desk. "Do you have any extra rooms tonight?"

A ponytailed attendant smiles, taps the keyboard, then frowns. "We are all sold out."

"Are you sure?"

"So sorry. But yes, I'm sure."

I return to my chair. Surely, Veronica can't go all night long.

But at two thirty, it's still me and my book.

I yawn, barely able to stay awake anymore. My eyes flutter closed, and before I know it, I sit bolt upright at five thirty, greeted by the blazingly bright morning sun, and a massive crick in my neck, having spent the night curled up in an uncomfortable emerald green leather chair in the lobby of my hotel.

But it was worth it, evidently, I learn when I return to the room, greeted by a contrite but glowing Veronica.

"I'm so sorry I didn't fetch you. We were busy, and then we were busy again, and then I crashed, and I'm the worst friend in the world."

"Don't even think twice about it. I'm glad you were —wink, wink—busy," I say as we pack.

"I'm terrible. But you truly are a saint," Veronica declares as she stuffs clothes and makeup hastily in her bag.

"I'll be awaiting my official canonization any day, then."

Sitting back on her heels, she tugs the zipper with vigor, sealing her suitcase. She grabs her phone when it buzzes, then scans the message as I check and double-check that my passport is secure.

"Eek! The airline gave me a first-class upgrade."

"Lucky you."

She dances her way over to me, her eyes twinkling. "No. Lucky you. It's my gift to you for the valorous act of compassion you performed last night for me."

"No, I can't," I say, but I can, I truly can.

"I insist."

Twisting my tired arm won't be hard. "Really?"

"Take it. You deserve it."

All the way to the airport, Veronica tells me it was the best sex of her life. The best night of her life. The most interesting man she's ever met. She can't stop smiling. She can't stop beaming. "I'm happy, Elise. I'm ridiculously happy."

*Happy.*

What does it take to be happy anymore?

"Will you see him again?"

She laughs, shaking her head. "Doubtful. He's a boat captain in Denmark. I'm a candy-maker in France." Veronica runs a handful of popular artisan candy shops in Paris. "Besides, I don't need something to last to make me happy. I don't even need something to happen twice for me to enjoy it. Though, let me tell you, it was three times."

She's brimming over in the morning-after glow of great sex, buzzed on the lingering effects. I know too well what that's like, to be so blissed out that anything feels possible.

Turning, I stare out the window as the brick buildings and cobbled pedestrian streets give way to sleeker, more modern structures. I wonder how I should live my life now—a year after everything with Eduardo fell to pieces. Like Veronica, daring and wild? Or perhaps like me, the woman who lubricated a magical kind of night for a friend?

She's glowing. I'm thinking.

She's bubbling. I'm contemplating.

Who do I want to be?

When we reach the airport, make our way through

security, and step onto the plane, I sink into a plush, first-class seat.

It's so lush, so comfortable, and so precisely what I need.

I sigh happily, then laugh at myself. My friend is on cloud nine from orgasms. I'm walking on air from a leather seat.

Maybe last night wasn't such a loss after all. Maybe it was the start of starting over.

As a spectator.

As the sidekick.

As the friend who sleeps in the lobby so one of her besties can seize the day.

Yes, that's the better path for me. I have a business to run, a company to shore up, and a heart that I won't let out to play again. Life is for living well, not loving well.

I shut my eyes, briefly wondering if I'll ever see the man from the dock again.

The world doesn't work like that. You only see a naked handstander once.

That's just how life is.

# 4

# CHRISTIAN

*The night they were supposed to meet*

Win some. Lose some.

After an hour at The Jane, during which I engage in several heated discussions with other patrons about football, European-style; the best digital currency to invest in; and finally, the astounding versatility of eggs as a food topping—you can slap a fried egg on rice, pizza, a crepe, noodles, and so on—I resign myself to reality.

My little mermaid isn't coming.

Grabbing my pint, I down the remainder of the beverage and set the glass on the bar.

Maybe one last scan.

I survey the sleek bar with its chaise lounges and royal-blue couches. Tall men and women have poured themselves over the cushions, clinking glasses, chatting, flirting.

None look like the woman from the boat.

"*C'est la vie*," I tell the bartender.

He nods knowingly and repeats the saying. He has no clue what it means to me in this moment. But he's a good bartender, so he agrees.

Maybe it was foolish to think she might actually show up. The woman did add a *perhaps* before she said she'd see me. There's hardly a more noncommittal word in the English language than perhaps.

My gaze drifts to my phone by force of habit, as if there might be a text telling me she's late, but she promises to be here any minute. As if she'll say *I can't wait to see your sexy arse*.

But of course she sends no text because *she doesn't have my number*.

This was just a lark.

I toss some money on the counter and head out. I stroll along the canal, through Nyhavn, passing the colorful homes, including the one where Hans Christian Andersen penned his most famous fairy tales, like "The Princess and the Pea." Across the bridge, I wind my way through the quieter streets to my place.

I bought this modern two-bedroom home when I had business in this city relatively often. But I also liked being near my mum, and my grandfather too, especially since, as tough as he is, his health has been touch and go lately. In my humble opinion, it's his spirits that are bringing him down. They've dampened, understandably, since our grandmother passed away a year ago.

I slide the key in the lock, go in, and flick on a hall light to find Erik sprawled out on the couch, snoozing.

A glossy magazine is in his hands, sliding through his fingers, as if he was reading it mere moments ago. It falls to the hardwood where it hits with a gentle thud. He flinches, as if he's about to wake up, but instead flips to his side, still snoozing.

Quietly, I pad over to him and pick it up, since I'm not fond of messy homes. He's been reading an article on Copenhagen nightlife, and I peruse it quickly.

*The Jane, not to be confused with the little bistro Jane, is a happening joint.*

I groan as I toss the magazine on the coffee table.

*Jane.*

I bet that's where the little mermaid went tonight. Jane, not *The Jane.*

I can't believe I forgot about that little eatery and its nefarious plans to trip me up tonight. Damn. I'm losing my touch.

I shrug as I head to my room. What can you do?

I'll never see her again.

* * *

After I brush my teeth, my phone buzzes.

A bolt of tension shoots through me. Phone calls this late can only bring bad news. Perhaps it's Grandfather. Perhaps it's another frantic call from my mum that his health has taken a turn for the worse.

But the number is a Paris one. I answer it.

"Is this Christian Ellison?" It's a man's voice, a French accent to his English.

"Yes, this is he. How can I help you?"

"This is Jean-Paul at the Capstone Language Institute. Sorry for the late hour, but your name was given to me by Griffin Thomas," he says, mentioning my good friend.

Griffin and I went to school together in London, and he recently moved to Paris. He's been telling me to put my language skills to use. Griffin says it's an affront to the universe if I don't share them, so he must have passed on my name. I didn't learn six languages to not use them. I studied my arse off from the age of five so I'd never be without the ability to communicate.

"Tell me more," I say to the man on the phone.

Jean-Paul gives me the basics of the assignment. A large multi-national company with business interests across the globe is hosting a conference in Paris, and yada, yada, yada. That's all I need to know. *Business, multinational, partnerships*—those words whet my appetite. Besides, my calendar has been mockingly empty, longing to be filled.

"Can I lure you out of retirement?"

He barely needs to ask once. "When does it start? A week?"

"Monday," he says, his voice nervous. "I'd need you on a plane to Paris tomorrow. The eleven a.m. flight."

"Consider it done."

A burst of excitement zips through me. I have something to do. Somewhere to be. I text my mates that I'll miss drinks tomorrow night, and I'm not bothered when they text back that there's no way in hell they'll let me cash in another time.

The next morning, I sling a duffel bag on my shoulder and head to the airport.

When I retired a year ago, flush with cash from the

sale of most of my holdings, I imagined that my greatest goal would be to do what I wanted any second of the day.

To live life to the fullest.

To climb mountains, sail the seas, wander the streets and take leisurely lunches, meet lovely and brilliant women and entertain them with my tongue and other talents all night long. Don't get me wrong. I've enjoyed all of it, yet there's nothing quite as fulfilling as, well, filling my days.

As I head down the Jetway and onto the plane, I glance briefly to the left, checking out the first-class section. That used to be my stomping ground. First-class everywhere, a champagne and caviar lifestyle. I wouldn't complain about a cushy seat in one of the first rows, but since Capstone is flying me over, I'll spend the short flight in economy.

I turn the other way to find my seat, then stop in my tracks, the strangest thought flickering through my head. I whip my gaze back, peering at the second row in first class. A petite brunette with black cat eye glasses reminds me vaguely of the woman from yesterday. She's sound asleep, and I can only see her profile. But it scratches an itch in my mind, and I can't stop wondering if it's her.

"Excuse me, sir. Can I help you find your seat?" The flight attendant asks kindly but pointedly too. *Move along. There's nothing to see here.*

I point to the back of the jet. "I'm all good."

I shake away the crazy thoughts. My brain is playing tricks on me. That's not her, and there's no way I'll see her again, no way she'd be on the same plane.

As we fly over Germany, I let the date that never was fall out of my head.

I don't think about her any longer.

* * *

For the next year, I enjoy the hell out of having something to do nearly every day. Something I love. Something that keeps me more than busy—something that brings me pleasure.

*Talking.*

I've always loved to talk. To tell stories. To chat, whether with strangers or friends, business partners or adversaries, my family or the women I've dated and sometimes become entangled with. Talking about anything and nothing is one of my greatest pleasures.

Griffin was right. I do love translating, and I love Paris, and I love the life I've carved out as I bounce from assignment to assignment, translating for French, Danish, Swedish, and other companies that need my expertise, picking up jobs as I want them, enjoying evenings out with friends in the City of Lights.

The best part? My brother, Erik, moves to Paris with his wife, and works feverishly to expand the firm and strike new deals. That keeps me occupied too, since he lets me dip my fingers in the pie now and then and help him bake the partnerships to the right temperature.

I don't mind helping him. He's the reason I have two homes, a fat bank account, and the choice to live my life the way I want. I owe all my success to him.

It's a brilliant year as I turn 30, with one exception.

For one dark month, I return to Copenhagen to

mourn the loss of my grandfather when he passes away at the ripe old age of ninety.

We cry, and we comfort our mum, but mostly we remember how good he was at being human.

Then, I see her again.

# 5

## ELISE

*Nearly three years ago . . .*

*Stop and Smell the Days blog*

***December 12: The enticing scents of cedar and smoke, and being swept off your feet***

My lovelies . . .

We must talk about the allure of cedar. Do you know the way your senses tingle when you inhale that fresh, woodsy scent?

You picture newness. You *feel* first times.

That's where I am now, in the throes of early

enchantment since I've met someone. I met him at a bistro in The Marais when I was dining alone. He was too. Isn't there something about a man who dines alone that intrigues you? It intrigued me. It takes a certain confidence to stroll into an establishment and ask for a table, party of one.

His eyes strayed toward me from time to time as he drank his wine. He looked at me with such intensity that my skin warmed all over.

When at last he rose, walked over, and asked if he could join me, my nose tingled as I inhaled him. His scent, cedar and a hint of sweet smoke, was the kindling. I was the match. He was nighttime and the notion that a feeling can last forever.

After that night, I dabbed some "Daring" behind my ears. It's a brand-new scent, and it'll always remind me how I felt when I met him.

Like fire and hot urgent kisses.

Until the next time. May your nights be daring too.


Yours in noses,
  A Scentsual Woman

# 6

# ELISE

*Present day*

My heels clack against the sidewalk as I exit the metro in Oberkampf, on my way to meet friends. I wonder what Joy's new beau will be like. He seems like a stand-up fellow, so enchanting.

But I thought that about Eduardo too. We were all enchanted by him, including my followers, from back when I used to weave stories about him into my perfume blog—a blog I rarely write anymore. He'd cast a spell far and wide, across continents.

Flicking memories of him away, I stroll past Annalise & Charlie, doing a quick scan of the windows at one of my favorite boutiques. My gaze lands on a pair of candy-pink shoes with a strap over the instep.

"I'll be back for you," I whisper to the shoes, because shoes can't hurt your heart.

When I reach the hotel, the doorman nods in greeting, swinging open the door with *Hotel Particulier Tenth* calligraphed across the gleaming glass. I'm early, and that's by design. I say hello to the owner, Armand, who's working at the front desk. He's also a new client.

He beams. "Elise, to what do we owe the pleasure of seeing you here tonight?"

I bring my finger to my lips. "Shh. It's a best-kept secret."

He wiggles his eyebrows. "Yes, I love our marketing tagline."

This small partnership could pave the path to a bigger one. Armand's business partner is expanding a luxury chain across Europe, and I hope to secure a meeting with him. He's being courted by several agencies, including the Thompson Group, the same company I lost two of my clients to more than a year ago. That was my fault—my work focus had strayed during my marriage to Eduardo and the fallout after his death.

This time around, I plan to fight harder.

I say goodbye to Armand and walk through to an enclosed courtyard. Lush trees climb high, and ivy crawls sensually along the white walls. Strings of lights cascade from the branches of the trees, turning the bar into a glittery adult fairyland. The low beat of a bass thumps from the sound system, an enticing aural embrace.

A few minutes later, my redheaded friend arrives, and I say hello. By her side is the tall, dark-haired, handsome British man who's captured her attention and her heart since she's been in Paris.

Joy makes the requisite intros.

"So, this is the woman who says days should be eaten," Griffin remarks, a twinkle in his blue eyes.

"So, this is the man who's so enchanted my friend." I give him a look over the top of my glasses.

He wraps an arm around Joy, possessively. "The enchantment is entirely mutual."

The way he looks at her stirs something inside me. It's a reminder that love doesn't have to be tainted. He stares at her with adoration, but respect too. It's such a missing ingredient in some relationships, and I can see he has an abundance of it.

We chat briefly about his work, the hotel, the city. He seems honest enough. I shoot him an approving nod. "You've passed my test for the night."

He exhales heavily. "Whew. I was worried."

Joy laughs and grips his shoulder. "By the way, have I told you Elise is in charge of all the inquisitions in my life?"

"No. I'm in charge of the fun," I correct, laughing too.

Footsteps crunch on the stone path behind me, and a man's voice drifts across the sultry night air, his accent British. "Fun? Did someone say fun? I believe that's my middle name."

I turn to see a strikingly handsome man striding across the patio to join us. Well, I do believe I'll be enjoying the eye candy tonight. He's tall, with legs that go on for days, a broad chest, and a face that ought to grace magazine ads with those carved cheekbones. I must enlist him to sell something. To sell everything in the world. I'd buy it all.

"Elise, let me introduce you to my mate, Christian.

Feel free to ignore any and everything that comes out of his mouth. I know I do," Griffin says, and we shake hands.

Christian claps him on the back. "The sentiment is fully reciprocated."

"We work together. He's a translator too, specializing in the Scandinavian languages."

*Scandinavian.*

A memory from a year ago sits up.

Something about Christian feels oddly familiar, as if he's someone I almost met.

That would be crazy though. Besides, I wasn't close enough to get a good look at the naked man's face. And what a face this man has. "Are you from Denmark?"

"Born in Copenhagen, raised in London."

"That's quite a combo—a Dane with a British accent."

His eyebrows wiggle naughtily. "That makes me the best of both worlds."

Oh, I like my flirty Danish Brit. I like him a lot. He's going to make my evening so entertaining.

Joy and Griffin grab a spot on a nearby couch, entangling themselves with each other.

"I adore Copenhagen. I visited there a year ago and took one of those canal tours."

"What was your favorite part of the tour? Seeing the palaces? Hearing the stories of all our crown jewels?"

Perhaps I'll shock him with my tale. "Neither. I most enjoyed when the boat glided past a private dock, where a very fit, very muscular man was doing handstands naked on the dock."

His expression turns serious. "A little past the outdoor food market?"

I nearly bounce on my toes. "How did you know? Have you met the canal flasher? Is he the Mad Naked Handstander of Copenhagen?"

"Mad? No. More like fit, handsome, and well-hung."

"You've been admiring his package too?"

"I'm familiar with his equipment." His grin is downright wicked. Christian taps his chest. "That was me."

I don't move. He can't possibly have said that. A strange jolt hits me, like the past has whiplashed into the present. "What? You can't be serious?"

He gives a devil-may-care shrug that only the sexiest, most confident men can pull off. "I suppose it's possible there could be other devastatingly fit men who live on the canal in Copenhagen and like to do acrobatics naked to shock the tourists." He steps closer, his eyes lingering on me. "But would those men have asked you for a date? Would they have gone to The Jane, looking for you? Would they have been sad you didn't show?"

An unexpected burst of excitement flares in me. It's *him*. Christian is the man I almost spent my last night in Denmark with.

"You're him?" I whisper, shock still lingering in my words.

"I am. And I went to The Jane at seven."

"I did too," I blurt out, desperate for him to think I'm also bold and daring. "I mean, I went to Jane."

A smile curves across his lips. "I figured as much later that night. I didn't think for a second you'd stood me up."

I scoff. This man. I give him a you-didn't-just-say-that look. "Cocky much?"

"I am. But that's not coming from the cocky part of me."

"What part of you is it coming from, then?"

"No part of me at all. It comes from you."

I wait for him to explain more.

# 7

# CHRISTIAN

My little mermaid has swum back into my waters. I have half a mind to toss her on my shoulder and walk out of here right now.

But, there's the little issue of not being a caveman.

Unless she wants me to be one in bed, and we're not there yet.

For now, the gentleman is up, and the caveman is standing down.

"And why does that come from me?"

"Because a woman that bold, a woman who took pictures, a woman who shouted *bravo*, is a woman who's going to show."

A smile crosses her pretty pink lips. "Of course I wasn't going to back out."

"Damn, I wish we'd gone to the same Jane." Finally, I can enjoy a close-up view of the lovely lady who caught my interest, and the view is worth the wait. Her dark hair curls over her shoulders in thick waves. Her chocolate-brown eyes are warm and inviting, and her black glasses intrigue me. I've always loved a woman in glasses. While I haven't been pining for her for the last year—honestly, that would make me a pathetic twit—I am ridiculously pleased that our friends are friends. "And I'd like to know who the hell thought it was a good idea to have two Janes."

She narrows her eyes. "I'd like to find that person and give him a piece of my mind. I'd like to tell him I was *most* dissatisfied to learn of the mix-up."

I inch closer. "And if we'd seen each other that night, you would have been . . . *most satisfied.*"

Her mouth widens—those lips are so damn enticing—and she points at me. "You *are* cocky."

"But what if it's true? Is it cocky then?"

"Since that night has passed, I'm not sure we'll ever know," she says coyly. It's clear she likes the cat-and-mouse tease.

"Listen, little mermaid, I may never learn, but I intend to try. What do you say we make sure we don't miss a second chance at a first date?"

"Are you asking me out when we're already out?"

My eyes drift briefly to Joy and Griffin, tangled up together, whispering whatevers in each other's ears. "Shockingly, our friends are amusing themselves without us. Let's you and I have a night of it. Can I buy you a drink?"

"You may absolutely buy me one. In fact, I'm not even going to attempt to pay for a thing tonight, and I'm going to tell you right now that I'm not going home with you."

I crack up. "That only makes me want to test the strength of your resolve."

I set a hand on her back and guide her to the bar. The bartender signals he'll be over in a minute, so I turn my focus to Elise again. "So, tell me, did you enjoy looking at your nude photos of me?"

She arches a brow. "So, tell me, do you regularly flash the tourists?"

"Ah, so this is how we play it."

"Yes, this is how we play it. I want to know why you dropped your drawers. Is it a kink of yours?"

"Is it a kink of yours?"

"You don't get to know my kinks until you answer some questions."

"But you have kinks you'll share?"

She moves in closer and whispers near my ear, "We all have kinks. The question is whether mine match yours and vice versa."

A bolt of lust slams into me. She's everything I imagined she'd be that night. And I'm more determined than ever to learn more about her.

The bartender arrives and asks what we'd like. Elise chooses absinthe and I do the same. When he leaves, I lean my hip against the silvery outdoor counter, freestanding in the midst of this midnight garden bar. "Just so you know, the canal game is something my mates and I do for fun. It's high jinx, really. Nothing more. We do it for kicks."

"Like a party trick with your friends?"

"We buy each other beers based on our success rates."

"And is asking a woman out part of the point system?"

I shake my head. "I've never asked a woman out from the docks before." I reach for a strand of her hair, running my finger over it. *As soft as I imagined.*

Her breath hitches, but she meets my eyes like a cross-examiner in court. "I find that hard to believe."

"Why? You're not a woman lacking in self-confidence."

"But I am brimming with skepticism."

I rake my eyes over her. "You're brimming with everything I want to experience more of."

She nibbles on the corner of her lip, then shakes her head, clearly amused. "You're shameless in the way you stare at me."

"Why should I feel shame?"

"You shouldn't. I'm simply observing. You're one of those men who doesn't care if he stares, who isn't afraid to look."

"I like what I see. I'm not going to pretend otherwise. But because I like it, I want to know what's behind it. Even if you're a skeptic."

"Aren't you? A skeptic?"

"I am, and yet I can't help but believe in fate, since here we are."

She scoffs. "Oh please. You believe in fate?"

"You're telling me you think it's chance we met again?"

"I do."

I shake my head. "It's too random to be anything but fate."

She stabs a finger against the sleek surface of the

bar. "It's the very meaning of randomness. It's proof that the world operates on the power of coincidence. It's like when you spot someone from your hometown in a foreign city. It's running into somebody on a flight you haven't seen since childhood."

The bartender slides over our drinks, and I slap some bills on the counter then thank him. I pick up my drink. "But isn't coincidence part and parcel of fate?"

"Why do you want to believe this"—she gestures from me to her—"is fate? Don't tell me you're one of those hopeless romantics."

I laugh unabashedly, tossing back my head. "You say that like it's the worst thing in the world."

She lifts her glass, eyes me over the rim. Her tone is serious. "Are you?"

She truly seems to want an honest answer, not a flirty one, so I give her one. "No. I'm a realist, and realism dictates my feelings about relationships and the power of randomness." Then I toss out one more knot in the fate skein. "I suppose true fate would have been if we were on the same flight back to Paris the next day."

She laughs lightly, and I get the sense she appreciates that answer a lot. She takes a drink. "That seems highly unlikely."

I shrug as I swallow some absinthe. "The crazy thing is I actually thought I saw you on the flight back to Paris. I took the mid-morning one the next day."

Her eyes pop. She emits a small squeak. Her glass starts to slip from her fingers, and I dart to catch it before it falls. My fingers cover hers, and we hold it together. "Judging from your expression, I'm guessing you were indeed on the same flight. Wearing a blue shirt, lounging in first class. With these sexy-as-hell glasses on and your eyes closed."

She takes a deep breath and is quiet as a cat as she whispers *yes*. We put down the glass.

"Third time's a charm, then?"

"Seems it is," she says, her voice still feathery.

I raise my own glass. "Forgive my manners. We ought to toast."

"What are we toasting to?" she asks, recovering from her surprise.

I don't speak right away. Instead, I stare into her rich brown eyes. Wait until I see a spark there. A hint of desire, so I know she feels the chemistry between us. It's impossible not to feel it. It's real, it's crackling, and I'm not letting her get away from me this time.

"To fate."

She arches a brow, lifting her glass. "To chance."

We take drinks, then I lean closer as the music pulses louder. "I want to know how that tastes on your lips."

"You're forward."

"I am. And since our friends are friends, it's clearly fated that I kiss you senseless tonight."

Setting down her glass, she wraps her hand around my forearm, and I like the way her fingers feel on me. "Christian, you're literally the most handsome creature I've ever seen in my entire life, but you can't possibly believe that."

"Why not?"

"That's such a romantic notion."

"Who said anything about romance? Maybe I think

we were fated to . . ." I move in closer as I tuck a strand of hair over her ear and finish the sentence with a whisper, "*Fuck*."

She shudders, lifting her hand to her neck as if cupping the imprint of my touch as I pull away. She looks dazed, and that's a most excellent look on her. "You smell like coconut," I tell her.

"You're spearmint and liquor." Her eyes linger on my mouth. "It's devastatingly enticing."

"Let me devastate you in other ways."

She shakes her head. "You're too handsome. Too much."

I'm undeterred. I want her. "Elise, come home with me."

"No."

"Why not?"

"Because my mind is a blur of absinthe and spearmint right now." She raises a hand, brushes her fingers over my jaw, then cups the back of my head. I'm turned on beyond all reason. Brushing her lips over my cheek, she whispers, "And because you've wanted to kiss me for more than a year. Think how much better it would be if I let you have a little taste of me every now and then." She steps away.

"You're offering me a third date? Because let's be honest—this is almost like a second date, and you have seen me naked."

She laughs. "This is barely a first date, and only by chance. Maybe buy me dinner, and then you'll know how my lips taste."

"In that case, I know a little bistro around the corner that could rustle up something if I make a reservation for, say, eleven thirty tonight? Care to join me for a late dinner?"

"Are you always this persistent?"

"Only when I know I absolutely want something."

She's quiet as she raises her glass and takes a sip. She sets it down, her gaze never leaving mine. "I'm free next Friday."

# 8

# CHRISTIAN

One week.

She makes me wait one long, torturous week.

She has to know this only makes me want her more.

"And then we have this final set of paperwork to review," my brother says, when it's four more hours till I see her.

I stare out the window of the fourth-floor offices that overlook the Paris Opera House, then turn around, meeting my brother's gaze. "Yes, we should have this wrapped up quickly."

I'm in my brother's CEO office at the firm, plowing through the final details of Grandfather's estate, which will transfer control of his financial firm to Erik. After we sign this document, Erik will be not only the CEO, but the majority stockholder as well, with the final say over the company—as Grandfather, Erik, and I had wanted.

Even though I worked on a plum translation gig earlier today, speaking for a Swedish dignitary in town for a political consortium, I've spent a few hours with Erik too, though this hardly feels like work. Business has always come easily.

Well, since I decided to buckle down and focus ten years ago, thanks to the man here with me. I was a fuck-up in school, until Erik set me on the right path. And that path turned golden, paved with euros, millions of them, and I'm so grateful.

I stroll across the oriental carpet, and as I flop into the seat across from him, I glimpse a framed photo of our grandfather and his bride on the wall. The photo tugs at my chest. "Do you miss him?"

Erik sighs, dragging a hand through his blond hair. "I do. Even though we all knew it was coming, that still doesn't lessen the missing."

"Sometimes he felt like more of a dad than Dad." Our father has always been far too preoccupied with women to pay much heed to us. That's why Erik was the one who gave me a talking-to when I needed to buckle down at university. Our dad had been busy romancing wife number three then. Or four. I've lost count.

"I want to do right by Grandfather. Honor his wishes." Erik twirls a pen as he stares at the photo. "He built the firm, and I'm lucky enough to get to run it. I can't believe you don't want to."

I lift my hands in surrender. "No interest. It's all yours. Been there, done that."

"You sure?"

"I like playing around with it, like I get to do now and then. Dipping my toes wherever I want." I wiggle my shoe to demonstrate.

Erik gives me a dirty look. "I bet you'd like to dip something else somewhere tonight."

I smirk. "Guilty as charged."

"I really can't believe you saw her again," he says.

"Crazy, right?"

"Maybe it's meant to be, like Jandy and me."

I roll my eyes. "Elise called me a hopeless romantic, but the title is more apt for you."

"And on that count, constable, I am guilty as charged." He smiles dopily, and I know he's thinking of his wife. He's so besotted with her. He has a bit of a Prince Charming complex, and that's not a bad thing.

When he first met his wife, she was timid, he'd said. Like a baby deer. She'd had a crap upbringing, and her father was awful to her, but Erik took good care of her, finding her a job here that suited her, and she came out of her shell. Became a bolder, more confident woman. She depends on him, and he dotes on her.

He raps his knuckles on the table. "I hope she can make it home earlier tonight. I feel like I haven't seen her in ages."

I sit up straighter. This news surprises me. "Why wouldn't she make it home at a reasonable hour?"

"Oh, you know how it goes. Busy managing all these marketing projects."

I never thought Jandy was that busy in her job. *What if she's playing my brother for a fool?* I phrase my question carefully. "Is that so? I didn't realize we were engaged in so much marketing here."

"Right, but you don't get your hands dirty in that department. She'd been quite busy organizing our new campaigns, and since we moved here, it's been busier."

"Getting her hands dirty," I echo with a wink, since that sounds fairly reasonable.

"I like to get her hands dirty," Erik says, chuckling at his own joke. "And I'd like to break Dad's streak and stay married for a long, long time to one woman."

He and Jandy have only been husband and wife for three years, but judging from Erik's affection for his bride, he should easily meet his goal.

"No doubt you'll get there. You know I'm already disqualified," I say.

"And that's always been for the best. I know it was years ago, but Emma was never right for you."

I hardly think about my ex-wife, Emma, and those days when we drifted apart shortly after tying the knot post-university. "That's true."

"What about now? What are you up to tonight?"

"Me?" I tap my chest. "I have one date and you're asking me if I'm ever going to get married again?"

"No, you twat." He lobs the pen at me and I catch it easily. "Just wondering what you're doing with Elise tonight."

Maybe he can see through me. Perhaps it's painted on my face that I've been thinking of Elise all day. She's elusive. Making me wait. Perhaps that's why I want to see her so badly.

Then again, maybe I want to see her because everything between us sparked.

"I'm going to be having the time of my life," I answer as we return to paperwork.

Soon, we finish for the day, and Erik closes his laptop. "Good thing you own so many damn shares of this company, or I'd feel guilty tapping your brain for all this."

"Good thing I have a sick love of business."

"It is an illness, isn't it?"

"It's a right madness. Only matched by my bottomless love of the female form."

"Get out of here, you dog." He mimes tossing a ball at me.

I pant and trot off as if to catch it.

* * *

Elise saunters down the avenue, and I have the pleasure of watching her approach. There's an ease to how confidently she walks, even in four-inch heels. She's so fucking Parisian, and it's an insane turn-on, that *je ne sais quoi* of French women.

Her black dress hugs her hips. It's cut short, and she wears pink shoes with a little strap over the top of each foot.

She's looking off to the side, chatting on the phone, her hair blowing in the spring breeze. I imagine she's barking orders at an underling perhaps. Bet she loves giving orders. Bet she likes being given them in bed even more. Women like her who command a boardroom are often the ones who most like to give up control.

I don't require submission though. I'm not that kind of a man. I find when it comes to matters of the flesh, I'm omnivorous. She can ride me hard, or I can bend her over the edge of her desk. Whatever her pleasure is, I'd like to deliver it.

When she reaches me, she ends her call, tucks the phone in her purse, and looks me over. "You have a way of growing more handsome every time I see you, Christian. But I suppose the real question now is will you be more interesting than the last time?"

The gauntlet has been thrown.

# 9

## ELISE

I declined his dinner invitation.

I turned down his suggestion for drinks.

I didn't want to go to a club.

Not that I dislike those places. Quite the contrary. But they're designed to speed the path to stupid choices.

Good food makes you moan in pleasure. Seductive clubs drive you to dance too closely. And cocktails loosen lips.

I don't need my inhibitions lowered with a man this devilishly good-looking. It's always the pretty ones who have deadly secrets. I don't know what sort of cruel mistress the universe is to create devastatingly hand-some men who'll eviscerate a woman's emotions, but I do know she's the cruelest on this count.

That's why I picked something for our date I'd do with a friend.

We're going to attend a decorative arts show in an exhibition space by the Tuileries.

It's not even remotely sexy.

It's somewhere to laugh at the absurdity of things that you see. To wonder who could possibly want a thirty-foot-long, pink faux-fur-lined couch for the living room, or a mirror completely covered in seashells so that you can only see bits and pieces of your face. It's the type of place that has industrial pipes hanging from picture frames and masquerading as art.

Once inside, Christian reaches for my hand. "Can I hold your hand?"

Perhaps because I'm caught off guard, I say yes.

He wraps his big palm around mine, and I notice instantly how long his fingers are. How firm his grip is. And how soft his skin is. He squeezes playfully, then wiggles his eyebrows, as if saying there's more he can do with those fingers.

*I bet.*

Tiny little shimmers of electricity dance up my arms, and I squeeze back as we walk along the cavernous hallway.

"Anything in particular you want to see? Are you looking for a new chandelier with a crystal flamingo hanging from it?"

He points behind me, and I turn to see a large chandelier hanging in the middle of an exhibition area. A pink crystal flamingo dangles from the lighting fixture, exactly as described.

"You know what they say. A room isn't fully decorated until you have a chandelier with a little flamingo hanging from it."

"Speaking of chandeliers," he asks, "do you like opera?"

Tension spreads over my shoulders. I can't stand it, but I'd said yes anyway when Eduardo wanted to take me to *La Traviata*. I said yes because he loved it.

This is my chance to do things differently. To learn from my mistakes. Even though I've no interest in a relationship, and even though this is only fun, I won't be less than patently honest with Christian. "I despise it."

He hums his approval. "I knew you were perfect for me."

I nudge him with my hip. "Do you truly hate it?"

"With a deep and instinctive passion."

"Poor opera."

"Poor me for the three times my father made me go."

"You must have been a very bad boy for him."

"Come to think of it, I was officially the worst. And I'm glad you didn't suggest we go to the opera tonight. I could have mustered the strength to sit through it to be near you, but I'd rather not fake it."

I stop and put a hand on his firm, broad shoulder. "Don't fake it. Don't fake anything. It's better to be bluntly honest. Even if it seems rude, honesty is better." My tone is tinged with a plea, but I don't care if I sound like a beggar.

He brushes a curl of hair over my shoulder. "I don't have to fake a thing with you."

"Ditto," I whisper, and for a second, maybe more, the air between us feels charged, sparking with ions and electrons. As if we could lean in, brush each other's lips, test out a kiss. Set the exhibit hall to flames. I suspect he'd kiss like that—fire and power and heat.

But instead, we continue walking along the wide, carpeted hallway, surrounded by Parisian hipsters, including a man wearing jeans so tight they look like leggings and a woman with a red-checked blanket draped over her shoulders.

"Why does everyone wear blankets these days?" I ask.

"Why aren't scarves good enough?"

"Blankets should be for beds."

"But, to play devil's advocate, you'd look really fucking good in bed with nothing but a blanket on."

I shake my head in amusement. This man is brimming with sexual innuendo, and it's ridiculously appealing.

I stop in my tracks at a huge black-and-white photo with the word *#space* on it. I step closer, peering at it. "Is that the moon?"

"I think it is. And holy crap, they're listing it for two thousand euros. That's bollocks."

"It's not as if this person actually went to the moon and took the picture himself."

"They probably went into the national archives, grabbed a photo of the moon landing, and blew it up in a copy shop."

"I'm in the wrong business, if you can take a photocopy and sell it for that amount. I should get out of advertising and into the hoodwinkery trade."

He laughs. "I'll be right there with you. We'll capture cell phone shots of the photos of the great events in world history, blow them up, add a hashtag, and sell them at the art and design center."

"We'll be in the business of highway robbery." I

turn around to find a humongous chair made out of wicker. It looks like a thatched throne, and the back of it is literally ten feet tall, with a seat covered in a patchwork quilt of pillows. "Speaking of highway robbery."

"Ah, I've been hunting for a comfy new chair." Christian parks himself in it and pats an emerald-green pillow next to him. "Come try it out."

That means I'll be wedged against him.

There's no other answer but yes, please.

I drop down next to him in the seat, and he slides an arm across my lower back, wrapping his hand possessively around my waist. "You fit nicely next to me," he says softly, his eyes roaming over my face.

A burst of desire shimmies down my body. "You're constantly trying to get close to me."

He leans in, running his nose along my neck. I stifle a whimper as he sniffs, saying, "You're right. I am. I find you fascinating and irresistible. Maybe you could stop resisting me."

A smile spreads rapidly, and I lean a little closer, *want* a little more. "I'll see what I can do about that," I tease, but I'm not giving in easily.

"Good. You do that."

Before I risk draping a leg over his, wrapping an arm around him, or slamming my lips to his, I pat the hard chair. "What do you think this monstrosity costs?"

He pops up, strides over to the beanpole of a man running the booth, and asks. When he returns to me, he offers a hand, pulling me up from the chair and tugging me nearly flush against him.

In a low, sultry voice, he whispers, "This can be

yours for a cool twenty-two-and-a-half-thousand euros."

He doesn't blink. He says it as if he would seriously consider it. I crack up, so loud I need to cover my mouth with my hands. In between breaths, I ask, "Does it come with the pillows?"

He shakes his head, a forlorn look in his ice-blue eyes. "Sadly, it does not."

Raising my chin haughtily, I answer. "Pssh. Then I don't want it."

We leave the chair and wander around some more.

"How was your week?" he asks, and the normalcy of the question gives me pause. He asks it with ease, as if we're used to the simple back and forth of "how was your day" and "what's for dinner."

"Busy. I was working on some new pitches for potential business at the ad agency I own."

He asks more questions about my agency, and I share a few details then inquire about his day.

"Busy too. I had a translation job for a bigwig. That was a lot of fun. And then I helped my brother with a few projects. But mostly I spent a good portion of the week wondering if this beautiful Frenchwoman was going to let me kiss her tonight."

I smile. "I'm only half French."

"Which half?" he says, a little impishly.

"Which half of you is British?"

"My cock, of course."

"My tits are French, then," I reply. Two can play at that game.

His eyes drift to my chest. "I love French," he says, lingering on them.

"Oh please," I say, and he refocuses, meeting my eyes. "My parents are French, but I was born in America and raised in Manhattan. I have dual citizenship."

"Do you feel more French or American?"

The question is a good one, and I've pondered it many times over the years. We grew up in the heart of the Upper East Side, speaking only French at home, as my parents wanted me to be bilingual. But my cultural touchstones were all American. "I feel like I straddle both worlds. What about you? Do you feel more Danish or British?"

"Would it be completely lame if I answered the same? I grew up in England for the most part, but I'm close to my mum and to my Danish relatives, so I'd have to say both."

I'm glad he answered from the heart and not from his British cock. I like the teasing, but I like more knowing who he is. "I feel at home being both too."

He takes my hand again, and another whoosh rushes through me. It lasts longer, spreads further.

"But would you feel more at home if you had *that*?" His tone is intensely serious. He grabs me by the shoulders and spins me around, and for a moment, I barely register what I'm looking at because his hands on my shoulders turn that whoosh into a wave of something a bit dirty, a little forbidden.

But there's no time to focus on the longing since I'm taken aback when I see a bronzed, stylized sculpture of a gorilla head. It sits on a pedestal in an art gallery exhibit. Surprisingly, I like it. "Now that's actually a really handsome gorilla."

"It is," he admits.

"I'm not looking for gorilla-head art, mind you, but I could see that in my house."

"You could?"

"Yes, maybe if it was, say, three hundred euros. For the sheer conversational value of it. If I were hosting a party, I could say, 'Yes, I have a lovely gorilla sculpture.'"

"Let's bargain. Let's get her to sell you that gorilla head for three hundred euros."

He strides up to the woman running the booth, standing a few feet away. "Hello. Just curious how much that gorilla head is going to set me back?" He takes out his wallet as if he's truly about to buy me a gorilla head on a pedestal.

With her blond hair cinched high on her head, the woman offers a faint, simpering smile. "It's seven hundred and fifty thousand euros."

I expect Christian's jaw to drop, since I can feel mine coming unhinged at the audacity of such a price. Christian maintains a stoic face, asking, "Does it come with the pedestal?"

Blondie offers another faint smile. "We can throw in the pedestal for that price."

He claps his hands. "Right. How generous. Thank you so much. We're going to go out, have a drink, and discuss the needs of our foyer."

We proceed to have a priceless time wandering around for the next hour, laughing about the cost of everything, and when we leave, empty-handed of course, I'm thinking how wonderful it was to do something irreverent and not at all designed to end with us in bed. Given the fun we had at the garden bar, I'm not surprised we had a good time. I am surprised I let myself enjoy it so much.

But a part of me wants to know what he'd be like behind closed doors. A part of me wants a little taste. When we exit, I yank him close and whisper, "That kiss you've been wondering about?"

"Yes?" His voice is husky, thick with desire.

"Take it," I tell him, my eyes fixed on his. "Take it now."

That's all he needs to hear.

He slides a hand around the back of my neck, holding me. In his crystal-blue irises, I see heat and desire, then a blur of lust as I shut my eyes. He presses his lips to mine, dusting them softly. It's a beautiful first kiss. It's exploratory and hungry at the same time. His tongue slips over my lips, his mouth opening mine.

My mind goes hazy in a heartbeat, like I'm having a drink, like the champagne is going straight to my head. Trembles run down my body, and I'm warm everywhere. The delicious, tingly, liquid feeling tells me I will be replaying this kiss tonight, home alone in bed.

I'll be wondering what it would have been like if I'd let him do everything I wanted, if I'd let him reach his hands into my hair and tug hard. The possibilities blast before me, and I jerk him to me for a few seconds, feeling the press of his erection against my hip.

He lets out a sexy, hungry moan that nearly breaks me. A moan that hints at how good we'd be together in bed. And how dangerous that would be.

I pull apart. "Good night, Christian. Same time next week?"

He tilts his head, the corner of his lips curving up. "Are you becoming my Friday-night affair?"

I raise an eyebrow and run a finger down the first two buttons on his crisp shirt. "Maybe I am."

He hums a note of approval, brushing a barely-there kiss against one cheek, then the other, before he whispers, "I'll see you in a week, Friday-night lover."

I laugh lightly. "We'll see about that last part." I slide my hand into his hair one last time. It's so lush against my fingers. Any trace of laughter fades away as I tell him, with complete seriousness, "For what it's worth, it's not easy resisting you."

But I manage the feat and head down the steps.

# 10

# CHRISTIAN

Griffin is quiet as we run along the river. I chat briefly about football—my favorite team, and the club league I play in—but mostly keep my mouth shut, since he has a lot on his mind.

We're nearly finished with the run. I joined him, as I sometimes do, for the tail end of his run, logging in three miles to his fifty.

Okay fine, it's more like ten or twelve that he peels off. Whatever the number is, it's a fuck lot more than I want to run. But he's the one training for a marathon. I'm merely trying to stay in tip-top shape. I'd rather be skiing, but alas, it is June, so running it is.

When we're finished, Griffin checks his watch. "I'm going to go meet Joy around the corner then shower at her flat."

"Or you could skip the shower. Go straight to the good stuff."

"Thank you. That thought hadn't occurred to me at all."

I clap him on the back, my breath still coming hard as we cross the busy avenue and turn toward a side street not far from Notre Dame. "That's what I'm here for. To make sure you never forget the good stuff."

"Shockingly, I can remember on my own."

We head in the same direction, since I don't live too far from here either. Griffin's fallen into silence again, and I know that means he's deep in thought about the decisions he needs to make. Figuring now is as good a time as any to give him a piece of advice, I say, "You know what my grandfather used to say about hard choices?"

"What's that?"

"We usually know what we're supposed to do. It's all a matter of accepting the choice."

He arches an eyebrow and gives me a quizzical look. "You're being contemplative?"

I shrug. "I have it in me from time to time. But don't ever let the ladies know."

He laughs, shaking his head. "Right. I'm sure they'd have zero interest in your soft, sensitive side."

I shudder. "I will deny you ever said that, and I will deny anything sensitive I've ever said. And on that note, I should go." As we turn the corner, a red awning comes into view, with *Café Rousillon* painted in gold script. Chairs and tiny tables spill out from the open café doors onto the sidewalk, wedged close together. Griffin smiles widely when he spots Joy, and as I follow his gaze, I see his lovely redhead isn't alone.

And I suddenly have no interest in going anywhere. Joy is with my Friday-night lover. At least, I want Elise to become my Friday-night lover, in every sense of the word. "I'll revise that last statement about my whereabouts."

"Oh, but you *have* to go," Griffin says, with an over-the-top insistence. "Don't you have *so* many things to do?"

"Nothing on the schedule. Nothing at all."

We head over to their table as they settle the bill and rise. Griffin and Joy say hello and goodbye as quickly as new lovers can, and then it's my little mermaid and me.

I smile at her, enjoying how pretty she looks in her white blouse and black skirt. Work attire suits her incredibly well. She's powerful, but feminine. "Clearly, this is fate, seeing you again."

She laughs and rolls her eyes. "It's chance, Christian."

"If it's chance, you never know what chance has in store for us when it comes to bedroom activities."

She shoulders her bag and steps away from the table, leaving some bills behind. "It's a good thing I'm not offended by your crude remarks."

"It's a good thing I'm not offended that you mauled me at the design show the other night," I say as we leave the café.

"That was not a mauling. That was me finally giving you what you wanted all along."

"Oh, sweetheart, I want so much more than a kiss."

Her heels click as we walk briskly, passing a boulangerie that's closing up its doors for the evening, the faint scent of raspberry tarts drifting out from the shop. "How do you know it'll be worth it? What if it's awful?"

I scoff. "Sex? Between you and me? It won't be awful. It'll be magnificent."

"Will it?" she counters as we reach the corner, stopping at the light.

"It will."

"How do you know?"

I turn to her and brush a lock of her hair off her shoulder. A slight gasp escapes her lips, then I run my fingers down her bare forearm, watching as the soft hairs rise in its wake.

I look up to meet her deep brown eyes. "That's how I know."

I drop my hand, and she shudders.

"Where are you headed?" I ask.

"I'm off to the metro." She gestures to the end of the street.

"I'll walk you, and don't even think this counts as a Friday-night date. One, it's Tuesday. Two, it's a bonus chance encounter orchestrated by fate."

She laughs. "It's a bonus bump-into-each-other."

"It's the hand of fate, trying to get us naked."

"You think fate has a lot at stake in the prospect of our mutual nudity?"

"It should."

"You're relentless. Also, you're quite sweaty tonight." She eyes my T-shirt then the slight sheen of sweat on my forehead and arms.

"Does it turn you on, Elise?"

She shrugs coyly. "I don't know. I'd have to smell you to find out."

I stop outside an antique shop, where an orange cat lounges in the window, sleeping underneath a cranberry armchair. "You're welcome to smell me anytime." I hold my arms out wide, inviting her to sniff.

"I'm not going to sniff you right this second."

"Why not? Are you worried my sheer manliness would be too much?"

She laughs and sets one hand on my shoulder. "Christian, I assure you that your level of manliness doesn't deter me whatsoever." She lowers her voice. "Whatever you're bringing, I can handle."

I let out a groan. "Scratch the Friday-night arrangement. We need a date tonight. Right now."

"Do we?"

I answer by reaching for her hand and threading my fingers through hers. She meets my gaze, and her eyes seem to say yes as we resume our pace, passing a florist shop that teems with orange, yellow, and pink summer flowers. Her attention strays to the blooms, and she sweeps her gaze over the lot of them. She lifts her nose, inhaling them.

She likes flowers. *A lot.*

"Yes, we certainly do need a date night. Don't you think?" I say, returning to the topic.

She glances at me, a sly smile on her face. "You may be onto something. But I can't tonight. I have to work."

"This late?"

"It's only seven. Since I run my own business, I have to work many evenings."

"I'll just go cry by the river and drown my tears."

She squeezes my hand. "You do that. The river is a fine companion for sorrow."

I sigh, then square my shoulders as if shrugging it

off. "On second thought, I'll grab a bite with my brother."

"You have a brother in town?" Her voice is tinged with curiosity.

"Yes, he moved here a year ago. Around the same time I started spending most of my time here."

"I trust that means you're close with him?"

"Very much so. He's my rock, my best friend, the person I trust the most, and all that. I help him with his business, and he's basically responsible for who I am today."

"Why do you say that?" Even though we're walking, she keeps glancing at me, making eye contact, staying engaged. She's more interested than I'd have expected, given the walls she erects, and I like that she wants to know these sorts of details about me.

"He set me on the straight-and-narrow. I was a right fuck-up in school, pissing away my days with parties and skiing, with late nights and later mornings, until Erik kicked my arse and made me focus."

"That's great that he helped you when you needed him. What did he say?"

"He said, 'You're not going to win a spot on the Danish National Team for the Olympics. Or the United Kingdom one either. Time to get your shit together and focus on school.' Only he said it a little better, and more frequently, and with enough tough love that I finally listened. Besides, he was right. My marks were crap, my attitude was worse, and my future was headed down the toilet. I needed focus, and he gave that to me. I wasn't going to be a skiing superstar. I was only dicking around on the slopes."

"You like to ski?"

"Love it. But it wasn't going to pay the bills. He knew that, but he also knew there was a better path for me in finance and investing. If it weren't for him, I'd probably have majored in poetry or geology or whatnot. I had no clue, and he was the one who helped me figure it out. Some days I wonder if I really ever will be able to pay him back for all he's done. But then, he's never asked for anything in return."

"But that's how it goes with people you love, right? It shouldn't be about what you get. It's what you give. We don't always give enough. But that's what we should want to do with family, with friends, with the people who matter."

The way she says the last part—*people who matter*—makes me wonder if she might have given all to someone who didn't give back in the same way. If that's why she seems so adamant in her view now.

"I suppose that's true."

"He helped you because he loves you, not because he expected something. And I imagine seeing you succeed is probably his reward." She smiles warmly at me, and I want to kiss her smile, run my finger along her lips.

I smile too. "Maybe."

"Also, can I say that I can't picture you like that, as a fuck-up."

That makes me happy, that she can't see me that way. "Is that so?"

"You do seem to enjoy fun, but I get the impression you're incredibly driven too. I can't imagine you're focused only when it comes to getting me into bed."

"Don't ever underestimate my determination when it comes to getting you in bed. But, you're right. I worked in finance for most of my twenties. I was, admittedly, quite driven and quite successful," I say, a little sheepishly because I don't want to come across as bragging.

She arches a brow. "*Quite*?"

I place a finger on my lips. "I retired at age twenty-eight."

"So young. That's amazing. What are you now, twenty-nine?"

"Ha. I'm the ripe old age of thirty. I had a good run." I give a little shrug, though I'm glad she seems impressed. I shift back to her. "What about you? Any brothers or sisters?"

"One brother. He's six years older than I am. Forty. He lives in New York City with his family, his wife and two children."

"Do you see them often?"

"I try to go back to the States a couple times a year to see him, and my parents too. And my brother usually comes here in late summer."

"Are you close with him?"

"In some ways. He's always sort of looked out for me in a 'big brother' way, even though we don't live in the same country." Absently, she fingers a charm necklace with an Empire State Building on it.

I tip my forehead to the necklace. "Did he give that to you?"

She laughs and looks down at the silver building. "He did. He actually bought this last time he was here."

"He bought you a New York icon in Paris?"

She smiles. "He's been doing it since we were kids. He finds it amusing to come here and track down trinkets that represent where I grew up."

"That's sweet. A nice way for you two to connect."

"I think so too. I have quite a collection of New York charm necklaces he's tracked down in France. Though I'm missing the first one he ever gave me: a taxicab."

"Maybe someday fate will send it back to your doorstep."

She laughs and shakes her head. "Fate doesn't care about my taxicab necklace."

"So, your brother is six years older, which makes you thirty-four," I say, scrubbing a hand over my chin.

She cocks her head and gives me a sharp look. "Why are you saying that?"

I hold up a hand. "What? You don't seem like the type of woman who gives a flying fuck if I mention her age."

"You're right. I don't. I was just curious if you were trying to impress me with your arithmetic skills or mentioning it for a reason. That's why I asked."

I lean in close. "The reason is rather simple. I like older women."

A look of skepticism crosses her eyes. "Is this a kink of yours?"

I shake my head. "No. I like when a woman knows what she wants. When she's experienced some of the world. And when she isn't afraid to call me on my shit."

"Because you do get called on that a lot."

I laugh. "I do."

"You deserve it."

"I do deserve it. And this is why I like someone to challenge me."

"You would like me to continue being a challenge for you?"

"Yes and no."

"I'll stick with challenging. Also, unlike you, your age isn't a kink for me. I don't have a thing for younger men."

"But you do have a thing for me, don't you?" I wink.

We stop at the metro station, and our hands slip apart. She stops and stares at me, her eyes eating me up. I fucking love the way she looks at me. She parts her pretty lips and answers, "I suppose we'll find out."

"We will."

She steps closer. She doesn't give me a kiss though. Instead, she lowers her nose to my chest where my T-shirt is a little bit sweaty. She raises her face, and her eyes have that hazy, sexy look. "You have nice sweat."

I loop an arm around her waist. "We could get sweaty together."

"Are you always so relentless?"

Dropping my other hand to her hip, I yank her against me, her body flush with mine. "Would you like me to stop being so relentless, Elise?"

She looks to the sky as if considering it. But she wriggles the slightest bit closer, lining up against me. She shakes her head. "No. Don't stop at all." She takes a beat then slides a hand between us, resting it on my chest. She runs her fingers from my pecs down over my abs and stops at the waistband of my running shorts.

Her touch is electric. I grab her hand, press it harder against my flat belly. "Don't you stop either."

She meets my gaze, letting her fingertips dance a little lower, then lower still. "Like this?"

A groan rumbles up my chest. "Like that," I rasp out.

Then, vixen that she is, she slinks a hand under my T-shirt and lays her palm flat against my stomach. Her fingers trace my skin. It feels too fucking good in public.

"See you soon, Christian." Lightly, she grazes her nails down my abs, turning me on everywhere. "Can't wait."

"You're killing me," I murmur as my brain charges full-speed ahead, picturing getting her under me.

"I know, and you like this kind of slow, exquisite torture." She dusts her lips against my neck then nips my earlobe.

I grab her harder, yank her closer. "You like it too."

When she pulls back, she wiggles her eyebrows. "Of course I do. I love it."

She waves then heads underground and off to the other side of the city. On this side, I'll be thinking in great and lurid detail about her wandering hands, and how long I have to wait until they torture me once more.

## 11

## ELISE

The next night I receive a text, asking me if I want to go to a tea salon on Friday night.

I laugh out loud, writing back as I take a break from tending to the garden in my small front yard.

**Elise:** You're actually inviting me to tea?

**Christian:** Yes, since you're avoiding date-like things.

**Elise:** And a tea salon is unromantic?

**Christian:** I think it's about as unromantic as we can get. Otherwise, I could take you to the grocery store. But as much as I like you, I don't really want to go to the grocery store.

**Elise:** Why do you like me so much? Is it because you haven't had me?

**Christian:** Do you expect me to like you less after I have you?

**Elise:** Of course not.

**Christian:** I like you for many reasons, but you've made it clear you have no interest in romance, and I want to give you what you want.

As I sit cross-legged in the soft emerald grass at my home on a curvy street in Montmartre, I trace my finger over the message, letting those last few words linger. What do I want from a man? What do I want from *this* man?

I've told him I don't want romance. I've made it clear I don't believe in fate. I can't let myself go to those places. They are cities where I'm no longer welcome, towns where I can't find my way. If I went there, I might get lost and never be found again.

But what do I want from him?

I sigh, turning to the sunshine-yellow tulips that frame my home. They're bursting with color, making peacocks of their golden hues, their bright orange tones, their summer shades.

These flowers seem certain. They're so deliberate in their colors, so spectacular in their showiness. But I don't know how to capture that kind of certainty anymore. I do want *something* from him. But is it merely physical? Is it simply that I feel a delicious spark every time I'm near him? Lord knows the man drives me wild.

Being near him is a complete and absolute turn-on, and his flirtiness melts me from head to toe.

Is that what I want? A naughty, wild fling? Is that enough? Is it ever enough?

I trim the garden more, but as I ensure no petal is out of place, I'm not sure I have any answers to my questions.

Or rather, the only answer I have is a simple one.

I want him. He entertains me. He makes me laugh. He keeps me on my toes. But he also hasn't asked more of me than I'm willing to give.

I won't scoop out a portion of my heart or mind that can be stolen again. As a woman who slid into the full-blown madness of a wild, dangerous love not so long ago, I don't know that a fling could be enough. But I also know it's all I'll allow.

I want borders, and I bet he's a man who respects the boundaries on a map.

I grab my phone and write back.

**Elise:** I like everything you've given so far.

**Christian:** Fantastic. Then, would you rather I take you to the bank? I suppose I could see if the post office is open on a Friday night. Maybe we could pick up toiletries at the pharmacy as another option.

I crack up as I sit in the grass, tapping a reply.

**Elise:** You forgot laundry. We could do laundry.

**Christian:** Ah, but that sounds dirty.

**Elise:** Dirty, but not romantic.

**Christian:** I'm trying to behave. And look at you, being naughty.

**Elise:** I suppose I shouldn't wear that short red skirt I had in mind, then.

**Christian:** How short?

**Elise:** So short it should be illegal.

**Christian:** Can you hear me groaning all the way across the city?

**Elise:** No, but I suspect I'd like that sound. Where do you live? I want to picture you groaning.

**Christian:** So you can imagine me in my flat tonight? You dirty woman. I live in San German des Pres, just off rue de l'Ancienne Comédie.

**Elise:** That's a fitting place for you.

**Christian:** Why?

**Elise:** That arrondissement is quite fun. And I believe

fun was how you introduced yourself to me.

**Christian:** There's so much more I want to introduce to you.

**Elise:** I suppose the same is true for me when it comes to you.

And on that note, I head inside, set down the gardening shears, and curl up on my couch. There's something I need to see.

No, something I *want* to see.

I click on the photo album on my phone, searching the archives for a certain series of shots I captured a little more than a year ago. When I snapped the images from the boat, the naked handstander was merely an amusing—no, outrageous—sight on a tourist attraction. Like a photobomber, but for the canal tour. Now, I know a little of the man behind the nude acrobatics.

I like what I know.

Perhaps that's why a tinge of heat splashes across my cheeks as I click open the first shot. I *know* who that upside-down flasher is. I know him, and I like him. And I suppose as I hold my phone at an angle, then as I slide my thumbs across the image to widen it, I feel a little like I'm perving on Christian.

Okay, *a lot.*

But that feeling doesn't stop me.

No, it drives me on.

I trace my finger along his naked frame, wondering how everything looks when he's right side up.

When he's stripping for me.

When he's stalking over to the bed, aroused and hard, his eyes blazing with desire.

When he's pinning me, climbing over me, giving me what I imagined I'd have that night in Copenhagen.

And now, I truly am imagining him groaning.

Because I'm doing the same.

# 12

## ELISE

*Two and a half years ago ...*

*Stop and Smell the Days blog*

*March 27: The search for a wild and rare thing indeed*

My lovelies ...

Just call me an explorer.

I've been hunting far and wide for a rare scent. It's from a lesser-known perfumer, and it's been dubbed Tangerine Wild. I've placed calls to my regular collectors, and slung emails around the globe in search of even a tester bottle. To my great surprise, I discovered it in a little village in the south of France.

I *might* have been there on a vacation with a certain man.

You know the kind of trip. Beaches, and waves, and sun that drenches you in its warm embrace. Afternoons spent in a bikini, sipping drinks, making the kind of eyes at each other that only new lovers can make.

Then, one fine afternoon, we ventured into a quiet corner of the town, where I at last found the bottle.

I'll confess—I squealed when I saw it.

Was it everything I hoped it would be?

It was everything and more.

It smells like honey and citrus, and even now, a few weeks later, I can still inhale the fine spray of salty waves and I can see a peach-mauve sunset on a beach where I lie on a hammock, peeling a tangerine, having no cares in the world.

But, I said it's everything and more for a particular reason.

It became more for me.

Tangerine Wild became the scent of something I'll always remember, when we wandered across the soft, sugary sand as the sun dipped in the sky, and he dropped to one knee.

It's the scent of saying yes.


Yours in noses,
    A Scentsual Woman

## 13

## ELISE

*Present day*

Sometimes, I miss New York City. The relentless pace fueled me. I learned how to jostle my way onto a subway, how to position myself on the platform to catch the right car at the right time. I could hail a cab and have it sliding to the curb, door opened for me, in five seconds flat. Hell, I could hail a taxi in the rain and barely get splashed on by the sky.

Sometimes, I miss the forty-yard-dash pace of the city where I was raised. The rat-a-tat-tat, go-go-go rhythm of the fastest place in the world, where we did everything in double time, especially lunch.

In Manhattan, we order, eat, and sign a deal before dessert arrives.

Not so in Paris with Dominic. He orders dessert, and we have yet to touch on the reason for this meeting as we close in on the two-hour mark for a meal.

It's a typical lunch in the City of Lights, where the world slows to a meandering pace at most eateries, including at this restaurant a block off the famed rue de Rivoli. White linen tablecloths hang crisply from tables, and antique gilded mirrors line the walls. Dominic chose it when I invited him out to lunch to discuss a business proposal. Since I'm in need of his services, I agreed to his haute cuisine. He's one of the most talented industry analysts I've ever worked with, and the highest paid too. I still lament letting him go last year when I had to tighten the belt.

"Would you like dessert?" the waiter asks.

I shake my head. "No, thank you. Just a coffee."

After the waiter leaves, Dominic leans back in his chair, stretching his arms above his head. "Okay, I am ready to talk shop."

I smile. "So glad to hear."

When we arrived, he said, *"Let's eat, let's catch up, and let's discuss business only over dessert. I'm dying to know how you are."*

"Tell me all about your proposal." He runs a hand over his mostly smooth skull. His bald patch has broadened in the last year, and his goatee has grown as well—his hairline is heading in opposite directions.

"I'm quite excited about this one. I think it'll be a great chance to make deeper inroads into a new sector, and I'm keen on the possibility of working with you again."

"You're lucky I wanted to listen. After you let me go unceremoniously," he says, huffing dramatically, as if it's a joke, but I wonder if there's a kernel of truth to it.

I smile softly, placing my hands together as if in prayer. "I know. Have you forgiven me?"

"We shall see." He winks, and I know he's hurt, but it seems he's not going to nurse it forever.

"Look, you know the reason I had to let you go is I lost some accounts to the Thompson Group. I felt terrible about it at the time, but it was the only thing I could do. The good news is I hope to rectify that now with a great new opportunity."

He stretches an arm across the table and pats my hand. "Yes, I know it was hard for you. I read your blog."

I jerk my hand away. I don't use my real name on my blog. I never have. "What?"

"Your perfume blog." His tone is matter-of-fact. "I figured out A Scentsual Woman was you when you axed me. I put two and two together from the things you'd said in meetings about perfume, and then I googled blogs and pored over some, and it sounded like you. All that stuff about that man. It fit you to a T."

My skin crawls, a creepy sensation as if someone's been watching me.

Someone has.

I suppose that's my fault for wearing my heart on my online sleeve, even though it was an anonymous sleeve and I don't have anything to be ashamed of. Since I learned the truth about Eduardo, I've scoured my blog and removed any story that chronicled my romance with him, though he was never named either.

But the fact that Dominic hunted around for me, maybe even hoped to find dirt on me, makes me uneasy. It sends a drumbeat of worry in my brain.

*Cancel.* I should abort this plan before it gets any worse.

But he's talented. He's saved me so many times over the years . . .

I ignore the flush of heat on my cheeks, the stain of embarrassment, and soldier on. "Be that as it may, I'm getting ready to pitch some new business, and I need a great analyst. I would love for you to come back on a project-by-project basis. I can pay you well."

"Go on."

I tell Dominic about a resort I'm prepping to pitch, giving him basic details without revealing the potential client's name.

When his crème brûlée arrives, along with my coffee, Dominic dives into his sweet treat with gusto, humming as he eats. "This is magnificent. This is stupendous. This is incredible."

I sip my coffee as he murmurs odes to his dessert.

"Are you sure you don't want some?" He shoves another forkful into his mouth.

"No, but I'm glad you like it."

We hold off on the business talk for another moment while he devours the remainder of his dessert. He plows through it, then sets down his fork. "I appreciate the offer, Elise. But I'm going to decline. I took a job with the Thompson Group. But thank you for lunch. I've always wanted to come to this place."

As the punchline to the joke that's on me, he drops his napkin theatrically on the table and leaves.

* * *

I'm fuming. Curse words in French and English and even the touch of Spanish I learned in college blister my tongue as I swear silently and fish out my business Amex to pay for his meal, resentment raging in every pore.

I fasten on a fake smile when the maître d' says goodbye, then I march down the avenue, pissed at how Dominic set me up, pissed at myself for sensing he was going to pull this crap, but still giving him the chance.

I growl in anger. This needs to end. I need all my mistakes behind me.

Screw Dominic. Screw him and his free lunch. I don't need him. I'll be my own damn analyst. I'll show him, and John Thompson too.

I walk, and I walk, and I walk, my heels clicking like bullets, until I hear the familiar sound of water trickling musically, and I inhale the comforting smell of damp stone.

I've done it again. I've wandered to the Fontaine des Mers at the Place de la Concorde. I square my shoulders and breathe deeply.

This was where I was scheduled to meet Eduardo the last time I never saw him. I waited an hour, calling and texting. Annoyance at him being late turned into worry over his safety, and that soon morphed into anguish the likes of which I wouldn't wish on my worst enemy.

The police called. His motorcycle had crashed. He was pronounced dead on arrival at a hospital an hour away. Devastation had flowed through every cell in my body, and I'd heaved with pain and tears for days and days.

That's where my story with him should've ended. The simple but terrible grief of losing a spouse. A widow at the ripe old age of thirty-two. A whirlwind six-month marriage that ended far too soon.

But I didn't even have the chance to grieve properly.

At his funeral, I met another bereaved woman. Her name was Diana, and she was also a grieving widow. His *other* widow. He'd been married to her at the same time as me, and Diana didn't know, either, that he'd left behind two wives. Two fools.

I raise my gaze to the water, watching it patter from the small bowl to the big one in a ceaseless rhythm.

I watch and wait for the clobbering.

For the pain to slam into me, like a cruel wave.

It doesn't come.

In its place, I feel something new. *Resolve.*

I don't have to play the fool. Not with men like Dominic, or men like Eduardo. I won't let someone have the upper hand again.

I grab my sunglasses and shield my eyes as I walk away from the fountain, stronger, so much stronger than I was that day more than two years ago.

And I'm going to be smarter too from now on.

I return to work, power through my projects during the rest of the afternoon, and head home. A shower washes away the remnants of the day, as I scrub off the lingering frustration from lunch.

I slip on my red skirt, then peruse my bureau with all the little bottles of scents, trailing my fingers along the cool black wood. I stop at an empty crystal bottle that catches the fading light from the early evening sun, reflecting it like a prism. It's Marchesa Parfum d'Extase, and it was a gift. A gift from many, and I cherished it.

I love it for what it represents. I hate it for what it represents. It haunts me now, even though I've poured it out and bleached the bottle.

Breathing deeply, I turn away, choosing none of the scents. Choosing a new path.

A fresh start to embark on this tryst for what it is—a neat, organized affair with a delicious man. There's nothing messy about Christian. Nothing risky. He's built for sin, yet safe for my heart.

As I head downstairs, I repeat my new watchword. *Resolve.*

I hereby resolve to play it smart and to make sure I don't ever get too close again.

## 14

### ELISE

When I arrive at the tea salon on the left bank, with its extravagant gold script on the windows, I think of my grandmother. The last time my brother and his family visited, my grandmother caught the train from Provence, stayed the weekend at the Ritz, and spent her days taking my brother and his children to all the sweet shops in Paris, from my friend Veronica's candy store to this salon, known for its fine selection of teas, hot chocolate, and madeleines. I can picture her clearly— her soft gray hair, her crow's feet, and her regal but loving smile as she lifted her fine white teacup while my nieces nibbled on madeleines.

The image makes me both smile and laugh, because it reminds me of how elegant this establish- ment is in all its fin de siècle glory, from the marble- topped counter display to the gilded mirrors. This is Paris of yesteryear, and it's so discordant with the thor- oughly modern man I find holding court at a corner table, a crisp white cloth laid over the surface. He's so casual and cool, in a sky-blue button-down shirt, a hint of stubble on his chin, and that sweep of blond hair across his head.

He's dripping with sex appeal, and he's the complete opposite of this belle epoque time warp.

I make my way to my Friday-night man.

He rises and drops kisses to each of my cheeks. These kisses linger—they whisper of what happens after midnight.

"Pleasure to see you, little mermaid," he says as we separate, and I sit next to him in a curved corner booth for two.

I arch a brow. "Little mermaid. Is that my nickname?"

"I didn't inform you of that yet? It's been your nickname since the day you checked out my cock on the dock."

A laugh bursts from my throat. "Are you the cat in the hat?"

"Meow."

"And why on earth would that be my nickname? Are women of the sea known for being oglers of naked fishermen?"

He reaches a hand toward me, brushing a strand of hair over my ear. I'm beginning to wonder if I have so many loose strands or if this is his signature excuse to touch me. I hope it's the latter. "Mermaids are sexy, and I met you on the water. Ergo, you're my little mermaid."

"It's not a Disney kink you have?"

"More like a *you* kink, I'm beginning to realize." He loops an arm over my shoulder and angles in to kiss me. He brushes his lips against my neck, but I change it up on him, turning so he meets my lips.

He groans against my mouth. Closing my eyes, I let myself slide into the feeling and enjoy the dizzying sensation of his lips brushing over mine. I savor it for what it is—a feeling, not a new way of life that cocoons me.

When he pulls back, his eyes have turned to fiery sapphires. The ice in them is gone. "So much for tea salons being un-sexy."

"And to think I was going to tell you a story of the last time I went to one," I say.

"Do tell. I like your stories."

This is a safe one for sharing, a smart one. "The last time I was here was with my grandmother and my nieces. This was a few years ago, before she passed. We brought her here, and she dressed in tweed like Coco Chanel, the height of French elegance. You did well in choosing a location that seems completely platonic."

"Interesting," he says, as if he's musing on the tale. "This place reminds you of your grandmother?"

"A little bit, yes. I suppose this un-date strategy is working."

"Is it?"

"Don't you think?"

His eyes appraise me, as if he's cataloging me. "Were you thinking of your grandmother when you walked in looking fit as fuck in this red skirt?" His gaze lingers on my legs, as if he's taking snapshots of where the bare skin of my thigh meets the hem of my skirt. His eyes stray down to my heels, then back up to the soft gray sleeveless top that reveals enough décolletage to hopefully drive him batty.

"No."

"Were you thinking of her once you saw me?"

My voice wobbles as I answer, "I wasn't."

His fingers drift from my arm down to my skirt. "Are you sure?"

I gulp and nod. "I'm sure."

"What were you thinking when you saw me here, waiting for you?" His eyes hold mine, his stare leveling me.

My pulse quickens. "How you looked."

"How did I look? Elegant? Stuffy? Unromantic?"

I swallow thickly, past the dryness in my throat. "No. The opposite."

A confident grin seems to tug at the corners of his lips, as his hand travels south. "You wore the red skirt," he says as he fingers the hem.

"I did. Do you think it's so short it should be illegal?"

"So illegal I want to be convicted."

"I suppose you could try being very, very bad," I whisper, leaning closer, buzzed on how our flirtation has climbed the heat meter tonight.

We're on the cusp of slipping into the realm of permanent arousal when the waiter arrives—perhaps oblivious to the eye-fucking we're giving each other—and asks crisply if he can get us some tea.

"Is Earl Grey suitably unromantic?" Christian asks me, laughter sparkling in his eyes.

"Yes, as well as the lime tea. Grandmother's favorite," I add.

He turns to the waiter. "Clearly, we need Earl Grey and lime tea, and that ought to save me from wanting to do inappropriate things here."

The waiter smiles with his mouth closed. "Very well, sir."

As he leaves, I nearly double over in laughter. "You scared him off."

"I have that effect," he says, then squeezes my bare thigh. It's more playful than sexual, and it's a little bit friendly too. He glances at my neck and runs a fingertip over the apple charm. "From your brother?"

"Last time he was here. We'd both laughed when he found it, since no true New Yorker calls that city the Big Apple."

"What's your favorite place in all of New York?"

"Central Park. Conservatory Garden."

"Flowers? Of course. I noticed you were quite taken with some we passed by the other day."

I smile, impressed he remembers. "The Conservatory Garden isn't just any flower garden. There are no cyclists or runners allowed there, so it's peaceful. I went there all the time as a little girl. It was my favorite spot in all of Manhattan."

"Do you have a necklace for the gardens?"

I shake my head. He presses a kiss to the hollow of my throat where the metal apple rests. "Maybe someday you'll find that to replace the taxicab."

I shudder and murmur *maybe.*

He raises his face and squeezes my hand, shifting gears. "How was your day?"

And that's not sexual at all. He asks curiously, his eyes locked with mine, never straying.

"It was . . . a day. How was yours?" I say, eager to segue away from mine. "Did you translate for the Danish king or something?"

He laughs. "A group of stockbrokers. It was great, and a wonderful reminder that, though I miss the highs of business, I like the freedom of my lifestyle more."

"In what way?"

"I can't seem to stay away from business for long, but I like doing it on my own terms. Translating for them gave me a fun peek into what they're working on but also allowed me to not get caught up in it."

"Did you feel caught up in it before?"

He nods. "I did. It's addictive. The rush and thrill of profits, of bigger and bigger returns on investment."

"Is that why you retired so young?"

He nods. "Partly, I think. I'd earned enough and wanted to live life on my own terms, but I also didn't want to be consumed by the constant pressure of the deal, and the next one, and the next one."

That word resonates with me. *Consumed.* "I think we're both trying to find more balance in our lives."

He arches a brow in curiosity. "Are you as well?"

"Yes, but not so much in business. I don't mind if business consumes me for a bit."

"Did it consume you today?"

The waiter arrives with a full tea service, a steaming pot, fine china, and teacups. We thank him after he pours.

Christian raises his teacup. "To red skirts I want to peel off."

I grin. "To blue button-downs I want to unbutton."

His eyes brim with mischief as he drinks. When he

sets down his cup, he returns to the topic. "What consumed you at work?"

I sigh, remembering Dominic. "I met with a former contractor for lunch, and he behaved like a complete jerk."

"What happened?"

Part of me wants to cordon off my business life from him, but I remind myself that telling him about my day, like I did on our first date, is not akin to letting him distract me from my focus. I give him a few details about the project I'm pursuing, mentioning it's in the travel sector. "I wanted him to do some analysis, and he basically said no, but thanks for the free lunch, and he's now working for the competition."

"He's a total fuckwit."

"Precisely." I take a drink of the lime tea.

"Do you have anyone else who can do the work?"

"I'll find someone." But that could be hard. Dominic has a particular skill, and as far as I'm aware, it is unmatched. I'll have to look harder.

Christian raises his cup to drink. "Let me know if I can help."

The comment is so offhand and casual that it throws me off for a few seconds. "How could you help?"

"You said the job was in the travel sector."

"I did."

"A lot of my holdings were in travel, finance, and the green sector."

"Interesting mix."

"They were my favorites so that's what I pursued. I'd be happy to offer any market guidance if that's what you need."

It's exactly what I need. "Really?"

"I'd love to."

I'm eager to toss out details right now, but I don't know that I should accept, because accepting would create more obligations, and obligations have a way of confusing matters of the heart and libido. I also don't want to entwine him in my business life.

"I can't take advantage of you like that," I say, though admittedly I'm intrigued by his offer.

We chat more about his background, and I'm fascinated to learn of the work he did, the deals he engineered, and the investments he made.

"Think about it. I'm not claiming to be the expert Domi-dick was," he says, and I laugh.

"I do appreciate the offer, but I don't think we should mix business and pleasure. Do you?" I ask, since it's not that I don't want his help—it's that I don't want us to confuse what we are.

"If pleasure's on the table, I like to mix it straight up with more pleasure."

"Of course you do."

"But keep it in mind, okay?"

"Sure," I say, though I know it's best if we don't commingle the two worlds. If one person is getting more from an arrangement, it becomes uneven, and starts to teeter under the weight.

"I'd be getting something out of it too. I enjoy that kind of work. You wouldn't be taking advantage of me —unless you wanted to in the bedroom. In which case, you have an open invitation to take advantage of me in any way."

I laugh. "Your business services and your bedroom services are up for grabs?"

"It's all up for grabs. But for the record, I would help you because I like you. Not because of any tit for tat arrangement. Though I like your tits."

"I like your tats . . ." I say, trailing off, then staring quizzically, moving away from the business offer. "Do you have any?"

"Don't you know the answer to that? You took my photo, little mermaid."

I quirk up my lips, feeling emboldened, my resolve turning into sexy strength. "I looked at your photos the other night, as a matter of fact."

"My full monty?" He raises an eyebrow playfully, as the background music shifts to Ravel, reminding me again of the belle epoque feel of this salon.

"Yes."

"Did you like what you saw?"

"I did."

"Did it make you want to see more?" He shifts closer, runs his finger along my shoulder, over my collarbone.

I shiver, and my bones warm. "Perhaps it did make me want to see more."

He drops his mouth to my neck, kisses me lightly, then nips my jaw. "I like that you're starting to see the light about getting under me and climbing over me. But I don't want to just fuck your body."

"What do you mean?"

"I want to know who you are, Elise."

"Why?" I tense. I don't want closeness. I'm not keen on emotional intimacy.

"Because then I can give you even more pleasure."

"Don't ask for my heart. It's not for sale." I cross my hands over my chest, as if protecting that precious organ.

He brushes his mouth against my neck again, his tongue flicking against my skin, licking me. "If you don't want me to, I won't even try to rent your heart." He nips my earlobe, and I drop my hands. "But I want to know your mind. I have no interest in sex being only physical. I want to know who you are and why you're here." He pulls back, his cool eyes locked with mine. "Why is it that you like this little Friday-night arrangement?"

I draw a deep breath and resolve to be honest with him. To clearly delineate the boundaries of my heart. They are uncrossable, and they are guarded with a wall so high he ought to at least know why he can't scale it.

# 15

# CHRISTIAN

I wait for her answer. I'm as curious about her mind and her heart as I am about what's beneath her clothes. You can't just make love to a woman with your body. You need to understand what's inside her head. Give her pleasure by knowing what she needs, where she's been, and what will bring her the bliss she deserves.

Already, I can sense Elise has had her heart broken.

She lifts her chin, a little sign of her toughness. "I like our arrangement because I don't believe everything needs to be over-the-top and all-consuming. I think sometimes things should be planned out and scheduled. Less heartbreak that way."

"Did someone break your heart?"

She looks away, and that's my answer. "Doesn't someone always break our hearts?" She turns back, her brown eyes searing into me. "What are the chances you can skate through life and not have any sort of heartbreak? Except you probably don't have any. There's no way anyone can be as happy as you are and have had heartbreak."

I scoff. "You really think I haven't had my heart broken?"

"Have you?"

"Of course I have."

"Who hurt you? I'll kill her." She holds up her hands, fashioning them into fists. I laugh, loving her fiercely protective side, and I'm not the least bit surprised she has one. It suits her.

"I think we broke each other's hearts, mostly because we drifted apart. That's a kind of heartbreak, isn't it?"

She nods. "I don't really think we should judge heartbreak. One isn't necessarily worse or harder than another. What happened?"

"I was married."

Her eyes widen. "You were?"

"Does that surprise you?"

"It does. You seem the consummate single man."

"I do enjoy my single life, but I also loved Emma. I met her my last year at university. She was in London on an exchange program, and we fell for each other. The way you can only be in love when you're twenty-one."

"The stupid, foolish kind."

"Exactly. But it felt like the real thing. She moved back to the United States, and I had a job on Wall Street, so it all felt like . . ."

Amused, she quirks her lips. "Like fate?"

I laugh at how easily she calls me on it. "I suppose it did."

"What happened? What cratered?"

"That's the thing. Nothing and everything. We didn't work out. We were married for about a year, and I think we both realized we were too young. We didn't really know what we wanted. I was getting started in the finance business, and she wanted to be a ski instructor and live in Colorado. That's not to say you have to want the same things to last, but we wanted opposites. She wanted an easy life. I wanted a challenging one. I'm not sure you can truly be with somebody unless you have similar ambitions, or a complete understanding of each other's hopes and dreams. Neither one of us possessed that."

"You didn't understand her, and she didn't understand you."

"Exactly."

Elise lifts her cup and takes a drink, a thoughtful look in her eyes. "Ambition is a strange bedfellow. I want it in a partner, I think."

"Me too." Sighing, I rub a hand over the back of my neck. "So, it ended. We didn't crater so much as peter out. We were like embers in the fireplace, then we turned to ash."

She inhales deeply, her eyes shining. "Sometimes it's all so sad. We try and try to come together, but so much gets in the way." She wipes at her cheek and seems to fix on a smile. "I still can't believe you were married."

"Bit of a shocker. But see? I'm not a total cad."

"I don't actually think you're a cad," she says softly, reaching for my hand under the table.

"Good, because I'm not. I've been straight with you

from the start. I'm not one of those I'll-never-get-involved guys. I think I'm more of a what-you-see-is-what-you-get guy."

"Are you? Because I could use that."

"Why? What cratered for you?"

She swallows hard and draws what seems to be a fortifying breath. "I was married too."

I offer a sympathetic smile. "Welcome to the divorce club." But when I see her stricken expression, I sigh heavily. "Shit, I'm sorry."

"The widow club, actually. And I wasn't the only widow he left behind."

"Are you kidding me?" My jaw hangs open.

"I wish. It was a whirlwind courtship. Four months, and he hid it the whole time. He traveled a ton, and he romanced me to the ends of the earth, and I had absolutely no clue. We were married for only six months after a short and very intimate ceremony, and he was gone half the time. I thought, silly me, that he was away on business. He probably was, but that business involved his other wife."

"Was she in Paris? Another country?" I ask, still shocked that her ex pulled off such an act. I've heard stories of double lives, known they existed, but haven't met anyone who's encountered them.

"She's Spanish, like he was. She'd been married to him longer. About two years. They lived in Barcelona. I found out at the funeral when I met the other grieving widow. She'd had no idea either. We actually wound up having coffee a few months later when she was in Paris for business."

"You did? What was that like?"

"It was . . ." She stares at the corner of the salon, as if she's conjuring up that moment. "Weird, but it was also necessary. We were both trying to move on, and I think we were both ready to ask each other questions. 'Where were you when he went to this conference?' 'Oh, when he said he was going to Madrid, he must have been heading to see you.' 'That time he said he was stuck in a storm, he must have had to go back to your home.' And so on. We sort of filled in these puzzle pieces that we hadn't realized at the time were missing. But they were."

"Did you blame her? Did she blame you?"

She shakes her head. "Neither. We both were in the dark. I felt strangely bonded to her for that hour we spent at a café."

I barely know what to say, but at the same time, a million questions zip around in my head. "So he lived in two places. Does that mean he was married in two countries?"

She nods. "And he used a different last name when he was in Spain. He had two passports for two countries, so I presume that's how he pulled it off. His 'brother,'" she says, stopping to draw air quotes, "called me after the funeral, trying to reassure me that Eduardo had married both of us because he truly loved both of us, and couldn't choose. 'Don't doubt his love for you,' he'd said, as if that was going to make any of it better."

"Was he really the brother?"

She shakes her head. "The guy was simply his best friend. Eduardo had called him his brother so it'd seem like he had family at our wedding."

"You must have felt like nothing he'd said was true."

"Exactly. That's exactly how I felt."

"Jesus, Elise," I say, my shoulders sagging as the enormity of that double-whammy sinks in. "I wish I knew what to say except that sounds bloody awful."

"It was." She squares her shoulders. "But you move on. You learn from your mistakes." Her eyes are fierce now as she meets my gaze straight-on. "That's why I like things the way they are between us. I like things prescribed and in control. I like that they're not consuming."

"I like it too," I say, because I like my lifestyle. I don't need to venture down a more serious road when the road I'm riding is smooth. "And I assure you, I'm not secretly married to anyone else."

"Excellent. No secret identities either?"

I glance at the ceiling, as if hemming and hawing. "Well, I do moonlight as a cape-wearing superhero with super strength and a killer grin." I flash her a smile that makes her laugh. "But other than that, I'm just me." I strip the teasing away and look at her earnestly. "But that's the truth. It's just me."

"Good. I like knowing where you stand. That's honestly the only way I want to be with someone right now, and it's probably for always. I won't go through what I went through with Eduardo again."

"Let's resolve to be honest. Let's resolve to not play any games, except in bed. Cards on the table."

"I'll put mine down." She spreads a hand on the table, as if showing a pair of aces. "To start, I want to make this arrangement exclusive. You and me." She wags a finger. "But no expectation of love or of laundry."

I laugh. "It's been exclusive since the night at the garden bar, little mermaid. There hasn't been anyone else. And I've done my own laundry for a long, long time, thank you very much."

"Excellent. Let's keep it that way."

I take her hand and run my fingers through hers, sliding them together slowly. "Can we enjoy this arrangement more fully tonight? Maybe explore the terms of it at my place?"

"What sort of terms do you have in mind?"

With my other hand, I run a finger down her throat. "I'd like to slide this top off you, kiss my way down your body, and lick your breasts."

She shivers. "I think I could sign off on that point."

"And under this arrangement, I'd very much like to peel off this skirt, slide my hand along your legs . . ." I whisper, my hand now drifting to her skirt.

"Oh God," she whimpers.

"So, a yes to that?"

"Yes."

"You say you don't want to be consumed, but I'd love to consume you with my mouth."

A flush spreads over her skin, and I want to take her out of here, strip her naked, and lick her all over. But I also don't want to stop. My hand slinks farther under her skirt, my fingers climbing up her legs. I can feel her heat as she spreads her thighs a little wider.

"Would you be amenable to that provision in the deal?"

"I would," she whispers, then she bites her lip as my

fingers reach the apex of her thighs. She's so fucking wet.

I slide my fingers across her soaked panties, the tablecloth shielding my busy hands. A quick glance around tells me we can pull this off. We're in the corner, the waiters are busy, and the nearest patrons are a few tables away.

A tremble spreads over her shoulders as I push the fabric to one side, then slip my finger inside her wet knickers. She gasps, parting her thighs a little wider as I trace her slickness. "Does this deal include letting me worship you with my mouth tonight?"

She nods.

"And does it include giving me the chance to fucking adore you with my tongue?"

Another nod.

My fingers slide along her wetness, and the hand that holds mine grips me tighter. As I reach that delicious rise of her clit, her grip on me turns bionic. "And under the terms of this arrangement, I'd want you to get naked under me, so I can help you let go of all this tension from your shitty day and your shitty ex. You can forget it all and be consumed by how I fuck you with my tongue."

"Christian." It comes out like a desperate, quiet plea.

I slide a finger inside. She digs her teeth into her lower lip, arching into my hand as she trembles. "We can arrange for you to come all over my face," I say, rubbing my stubbled jaw against her cheek.

She whimpers as she pushes against my fingers, trying as subtly as she can to ride me to the edge of her orgasm. She clenches around me, a sign she's nearly there. I inch closer, my mouth near her ear. "Would that work as one of the terms? If I could spend the evening with my face buried between your legs?"

She parts her lips, lets out a quick breath, then nods as she shudders and seems to melt, to turn boneless. A small sound escapes her, but she stays quiet, trembling as she comes on my fingers in the tea salon.

Her eyes close, and when she opens them, she's woozy and sex-drunk, and I need to make her look that way again. "You're wicked. And I want another."

"Greedy girl," I say approvingly as I lick the sweet taste of her off my fingers. Her eyes widen as she watches me.

I wipe my hand on a napkin and signal for the bill, and once I pay it, my phone rings. I have half a mind to ignore it, but I see Erik's name flashing. "Let me see what's up with him."

I answer it. "Make it good. I'm about to shut the ringer off for the night."

He sobs. "Jandy left me."

# 16

# CHRISTIAN

"Where are you? Are you home?"

"No. I'm outside."

"Outside where?"

"I'm at . . . I don't know. There's a bloody window planter on the building across the street."

"Okay," I say slowly, as Elise watches me with worry etched in her eyes. "Does the street have a name?"

He hiccups. "It's rue something," he says, and that's not useful at all, since nearly every street starts with rue. Tears are thick in his voice. Elise must be able to hear his end of the conversation because she sits forward, seeming cautious and careful with her movements.

"Are you wandering around the streets?"

"Yes. I see a streetlamp. Is that helpful?"

Hell, he could be anywhere. "A street sign would be more helpful. Can you walk to the corner and give me cross streets?"

He hiccups again, and it registers that those aren't

hiccups from coughing. He's been drinking. "Are you pissed?"

"I've only had three shots. But I fully intend on being absolutely plastered by the end of the night. We're talking uni-style bender."

I drag a hand through my hair, frustrated that he doesn't know where he is. "Your tolerance is crap already. Are you near the river? Sacré-Coeur? Notre Dame? The Eiffel Tower? The Louvre?"

"No. I'm near a church. It's across the street from a café. Hold on."

I wait, ready to go find him in a heartbeat. "It says Les Deux Magots."

"Stay there outside Les Deux Magots. I'll be there in ten minutes. We're only a mile away."

"*We're*?" He groans, and it's the saddest variety of sound. "Oh, crap. You're with your woman."

I glance at Elise. Is she my woman? I had my hands up her skirt until she came on my fingers. But she doesn't want to be owned.

She's no one's woman. She's her own woman.

Only, now is clearly not the time to address her status with my brother. Waiters circle, carrying trays of tea, and meanwhile, a mile away, my brother is drowning his sorrows over his wife.

"Yes, I'm with Elise, but I'm coming to see you."

Elise shoos me off, telling me to go.

"I'll go home," Erik says. "I don't want to cock-up your date."

"You're not ruining anything."

He moans. "I can't go home. I have no home. I'll get a hotel."

I take Elise's hand and lead her out of the salon, chatting with Erik. "You'll stay with me. Just settle down at Les Deux Magots, and I'll be there soon."

"Don't worry," Elise whispers. "Go to him."

"Bring her along," Erik says, sounding strangely chipper for a moment.

"What? You haven't even met her yet."

"I need a woman's perspective. Bring her along, and that way maybe she can make sense of what's been going on."

"Erik," I say with a sigh.

His voice is sharp and demanding. "Just, please. I mean it."

I cover the phone as we make our way outside. "He wants you to come. You don't have to."

She wraps a hand around my bicep. "I want to. Whatever you need."

Her smile is soft and gentle, and it's one of the first times neither one of us is teasing. The gentleness hooks into me and touches deeper than I expected. It isn't about the spark between us. It's about a woman who's been broken before, and yet she still cares for someone else. Someone she doesn't even know.

And I think I want her to care more about me too.

* * *

Fifteen minutes later, we usher Erik out of a touristy, overpriced café and into an English pub around the corner. The floor is covered in sawdust, and names are carved into the wood on the table. Erik picks at a bowl full of peanuts. His eyes are red, but dry.

He raises a pint. "Cheers. Drinks are on me. Let's get pissed."

Elise raises her hand to catch a waiter's attention. "We'll have two more, please, and another for him."

Erik smiles at Elise. "She's a keeper. Always trust a woman who'll drink a beer with you. Never trust the ones who thumb their noses at pints. Jandy hated beer."

Elise smiles. "Sometimes you just need a pint."

"I love her already," Erik says, smiling like a sad sack at Elise. "And I wish we were meeting under better circumstances, but I'm glad to make the acquaintance of the woman who has captivated my little brother." He stabs his finger against the table, grinning like a sloshed loon. "Did you know he said you were bold and daring the night he never met you? And so scrummy."

I roll my eyes, but I don't mind in the least that he's shared what I said. I've told her as much myself.

Elise laughs. "He was bold and daring. But let's talk about you. I wish you were having a better night." She stretches out her arm and squeezes his hand.

His lip quivers, and he nods. "Me too. But it's good to meet you. It's good to see someone who can make someone else happy. I thought I had that." He hangs his head in his hand, and my heart aches for him.

"Sorry, Erik. Tell us what happened," I say, after the waitress drops off the round that Elise ordered.

Erik heaves a sigh, shovels his hand through his hair, and says, "She's been working late, as you know."

My spine straightens, and red smoke billows out my ears. "I will string her up from her tits."

Erik shakes his head. "No, she's not cheating. At

least, as far as I know she has been faithful. She didn't say a damn thing about another man." He lets out a long, angry sigh. "She's been putting this together. This horrid plan to leave me. She claims she needs to be independent. Said she needs to be able to do things on her own."

I scowl. "This from the woman who was like a damsel in distress when you met her."

My brother huffs. "I know. She fucking needed me so much then, and now she's going on and on about how she needs to find herself. She said she feels like she has no identity of her own. That it's all wrapped up in being married, and since her dad was such a wanker, she needs a breather from being attached to a man. But not a breather—a divorce."

"She's leaving to go find herself?" I ask, trying to sort out the mess she's made of my brother's heart.

"Yes. And to do that, she wants the firm. Says it's all she knows. She needs it now. That's why she's been working late. To try to get it."

A chill runs through me. "How can she get the firm? You and I have the majority of the shares, and we're privately held."

He knows this. He should know this. That's how everything was set up in the trust. It outlined every detail about the shares of the firm, and he's the goddamned trustee.

His expression is sheepish. "I gave her a few shares for her birthday, in her name. She'd mentioned she wanted some independence, and I thought that would help."

"But not too many, right?"

He swallows. "Not too many. But she's been using her salary to buy up shares, it seems. From some of the other shareholders."

"Okay," I say cautiously. "But how could she have enough? Between us, we should still have a controlling interest."

He winces, and a look of shame crosses his eyes. "Because I also put my shares in both our names."

I squeeze my eyes shut, my body going heavy, like it weighs a thousand tons. He can't have done that. Please, dear God, make that a joke.

I open my eyes to find him offering me a "please don't be mad at me" smile, and how can I possibly be mad when the love of his life is leaving him flat on his arse and trying to steal his company? "Say you're kidding. That you're just going on about something else."

He shakes his head.

I try my best to stifle a groan, my frustration. "Erik . . ."

"We were married. She promised to love me forever."

Elise pats his hand and gives him a sympathetic smile. "Of course you thought that. It's normal to expect that."

"I believed we'd be together. Just like Grandfather believed in love, and that's why he left control of the company to his married grandson," he says, and of course I know about that stupid bloody stipulation in the trust.

Elise furrows her brow. "What did he do?"

I jump in. "Our grandfather was happily married

for more than fifty years. He was one of those true romantics. Very old-fashioned. His wife was by his side the whole time, and that's what he believed worked for him. That's what he wanted for the company he left to us. He put his majority shares into a trust, and his will appointed the married grandson the trustee. Basically, through the trust, that grandson has control of those shares—hence, control of the company, which was something we were all fine with. Our mum too."

"What if neither of you was married?"

"Then the shareholders—a board of directors, really—have control until such a time as one or both find true love," I explain heavily.

"That's like a fairy tale."

I nod. "It's exactly like one. His marriage was the definition of 'and they lived happily ever after,' and he wanted that for us. But it's never been an issue, since I never wanted to shepherd the company. Erik has been running it anyway, and he's been with Jandy for a few years now, so it all made sense when Grandfather laid it out. His expectations aligned with our reality. Over the last few months, we've been dotting the i's and crossing the t's on the paperwork governing the estate."

Erik takes a long drink and bangs his glass down. "And now I've fucked that up."

Elise rubs his shoulder. "No, you didn't. *She* fucked it up. She's not worthy of you, and she doesn't deserve your company, and we're going to do everything we can to help you sort this out."

"Thank you," he whispers.

Damn, she shouldn't be turning me on at a time like

this, but she sure as hell is, with her commanding tone and her deep concern.

"That means that among the other shareholders, she has the most control right now? If there's no married grandson to serve as a trustee?" Elise asks.

I nod. "Seems that way."

"She can make all the decisions?"

Erik nods. "And she wants to sell it."

I drop my forehead to the table and contemplate banging it a few times. I turn and look at him. "You kept that little nugget till the end, did ya?"

"Sorry, but there's a silver lining."

I raise my head. "Please. We need some good news."

"I talked to the lawyers. Some of her shares come due for renewal in three months, and they're the type of shares we can buy back as the officers of the company, and then she won't have majority control. We just need to prevent a sale before then."

I rub my palms together, shucking off my frustrations. "Okay, let's solve this, then. How are we going to keep Grandfather's company in the family?"

Erik snaps his fingers. "Why don't I go ask the waitress to marry me?"

I laugh morbidly. "You're not divorced yet."

He slumps down in the booth. "Oh yeah. There's that issue."

We toss around some scenarios for preventing a sale, and I'm doing my best to maintain a cheery vibe when Elise clears her throat.

In her brown eyes, I see a brand-new fierceness. "Yes?"

"Gentlemen, it seems you're missing the most obvious solution."

"What is it? Tell me. Tell us," I say.

"You don't know what it is?"

Erik shakes his head. I do the same.

"The marriage stipulation," she adds, making a rolling gesture as if encouraging us to catch up. There's a wicked grin on her face. A hint of mischief and victory in her eyes. "It only stipulates that a *married grandson* would control the company. It doesn't say which one."

Erik opens his mouth to speak, but no words come out. I'm not sure what to say either.

Elise points at me. "You could go propose to the waitress."

Erik laughs loudly, smacking his palm on the table. He points to me, a look of utter delight on his face. "Or you could marry Elise. For three months."

# 17

# CHRISTIAN

"Going to the chapel . . ." Erik's voice carries through my flat as he stumbles into the bathroom off the guest room.

"I do have neighbors," I remind him, since he's left the bathroom door ajar.

"Oops. I better be a quiet little crooner." But his next line about getting married doesn't come out at a lower volume.

"You're too loud." I toss an extra pillow from the closet onto the bed in the guest room.

"Let a drunk man sing while he pisses, will you?"

I roll my eyes. "Plastered, Erik. You're plastered."

"And sloshed. Don't forget sloshed. I am most definitely sloshed." He's quiet for a moment. "Oops. I pissed on the floor."

I grit my teeth. "You did not. You're thirty-three, not a fucking uni student with shite aim."

"My aim was top-notch in uni," he calls out in a

sing-song voice. He flushes, washes his hands, and emerges, looking victorious as he thrusts his arms in the air. "I did it. One minute and thirteen seconds. That's a bloody record piss. I told you I'm a champion racehorse."

I laugh because he's so ridiculous. "Yes, Erik. Good on you. You pissed like a racehorse, as predicted. Now, can you please get your drunk arse to bed right now?" I point to the mattress.

After Erik's ludicrous suggestion that Elise marry me, he proceeded to order a round of shots for the three of us, drink the trio himself, then propose to every woman at the pub. At that point, Elise called an Uber, and we dragged him out of the bar to wait for the Peugeot. Wily thing, Erik slipped into the corner market, grabbed a bouquet of flowers, slapped twenty euros in the paw of the cashier, and presented them to Elise.

"You'll say yes to me, won't you, love? American women are so much more trustworthy than the IKEA ladies," he'd said, slumping onto her shoulder once we piled into the car.

"Half-American," she'd added with a smile.

"I like half and half in my coffee. Do you?"

She'd laughed. "Of course."

"Which half of you isn't American?"

She tapped her stomach. "I have a very French appetite," she'd said, then winked at me.

Now here we are at my flat, where she's waiting in the living room. I told her she didn't have to come along, but at that point, we were all sort of in this together, so I didn't put up a protest when she stayed to the bitter end.

These are not the circumstances I had in mind when I pictured getting her back to my flat.

With Erik giving off fumes of Patron, he flops onto the bed, flapping his arms and legs in half circles. "I'm a snow angel, Chris."

"All you need is snow."

He sighs happily as he kicks off his shoes. "This is a perfect bed. I was meant to sleep in this bed tonight. I'm so glad my wife turned out to be a conniving bitch because it means I get to sleep in this stellar bed."

He flips to his belly and buries his face in the soft feather pillow, letting out a contented moan as if he's making love to the pillow. "Well, hello there, gorgeous." He raises half his face, glancing at me with one eye. "This pillow is my new wife," he whispers out of the side of his mouth. "Oh shit. I better propose to her properly." He props himself up on his elbows, gazing longingly at it. "Hello, pretty pillow. Will you please be my wife? Only you can save my company from that stroppy cow." He drops his head dramatically and cries out. "That sweet little cow. I'm still in love with her, and she left me instead."

"I know, Erik. I know, and it sucks royally," I say, tugging the corner of the duvet and covering him with it. "But get some sleep, okay? We'll sort it out in the morning."

"I'll sleep it off," he mumbles. "When I wake up, you'll make it all better for me, right?"

I wince, wishing I could make this pain disappear

by morning. Erik flaps his arm around on the cover like a fish out of water, fumbling around for my hand, I think. I smack his palm, and he yanks me close, hugging me. "It's a bro hug," he whispers, then laughs at his own bizarre joke. "It really is, Chris. This is the stinking definition of a bro hug."

I laugh too. "We'll take a picture and file it with the Oxford Dictionary."

"I love the dictionary. Do you have a dictionary I can curl up with? Wait! I have an idea. Maybe you can marry a dictionary, and then you'll be even smarter, and you won't do something right fucking stupid, like sign your shares over to your dictionary wife."

I clap his back and peel myself away from his zealous embrace. "I promise not to sign any shares to the dictionary."

"It'll all be better in the morning?" His eyelids float closed. "You'll fix this for me, won't you? I was so stupid. I was so bloody stupid." His voice starts to fade. "Make it all go away."

I don't know if he means the pain or the problem, but either way, my heart aches terribly for him. I've no clue what I can actually do, but I know I will try. "I'll do everything I can."

"Love you," he murmurs.

"Love you too."

As I click the door closed, I breathe a sigh of relief. At least he's in bed, and that's where he needs to be right now.

As for me, I'm not sure where I'm supposed to be. My plan for the night capsized a few hours ago—

though of course, I don't fault my brother, he's the one going through hell—then the plan sunk to the bottom of the ocean when he word-vomited the ludicrous notion that Elise ought to marry me. I wouldn't be surprised if Elise has only stuck around for the night so she could tell me she has no time in her life for these kinds of shenanigans.

She's not the remarrying kind.

Nor am I.

One failed marriage is enough for me, thank you very much.

When I turn into the living room, I find Elise has curled up on the couch, her shoes on the hardwood floor, her legs tucked under her, and she's flipping through a travel magazine. The bouquet of flowers Erik bought her is in a vase on the table, and I like that she tracked down a vase on her own and didn't let the flowers wilt.

She drops the magazine on the table and gives a sympathetic smile.

I smile back, and for the first time with her, I'm honestly not sure where we stand. From the start, we've been carefully circumscribed, with lines neatly drawn. But my brother's outlandish suggestion has knocked me outside those lines, and I've no clue how Elise feels about Erik's wild idea or if she even feels anything about it at all.

"I can't thank you enough for being there tonight. You were incredibly helpful."

She frowns. "I feel terrible for what happened to him. It's awful."

I sigh. "Yeah, me too, and it is awful. But I didn't

want to ruin your night, even though Erik really did appreciate you being there."

"You didn't ruin anything," she says softly, and this is the new side to Elise I saw tonight. She has a caretaker in her, and I couldn't have predicted that.

"And *I* appreciate that you were with us. I needed it too."

She gestures to the black-and-white photographs framed on my wall, then to the couch, a table, and the few books and magazines that rest on it. "I see your home is quite fitting for you. It looks as if everything has been imported directly from Scandinavian Design."

I laugh and sit next to her on the couch, glad her sense of humor is still intact. "I'm not sure if you know this, but being a dual citizen of Denmark and the UK, I'm legally required to buy all of my furniture from that store or from IKEA."

"A treaty, is it?" she asks, and perhaps I do know where we stand. Where we've always been—firing off words and wit, trying to impress the other.

I nod solemnly. "Jointly agreed upon by all of the Scandinavian countries. We can only furnish our pads with our most famous exports."

She points to the glass door that opens onto a view overlooking the arrondissement. "I kind of like that your place isn't terribly Parisian, yet you have that stunning window and what looks like a balcony."

"I can't complain about the view."

She doesn't respond. Instead, she looks at her watch, and slides her feet into her shoes.

Now *that*—that I understand. That means she's not

taking my brother's request seriously at all. I breathe a little easier, since that means we won't have to have a difficult conversation, but I breathe a little harder too, since it means I'll have to find another way to sort out the mess he's made of the business.

But it would have been such a perfect solution. Erik keeps the company. Elise and I have three months of fun and sex, and I get to spend more than just Friday nights in her glorious company.

*No.*

I need to stop thoughts like those. All they'll bring is complication to what is a nice and easy, linear situation. And that's the way we like it.

"I should probably go now that you've got him back home. Unless you want to talk . . ." Her tone is gentle, inviting, and I meet her gaze. Her brown eyes are earnest, stripped of teasing.

"I didn't intend to drag you into any of this, Elise," I say, reaching for her hand. And then, because I don't actually want her to go, I tug her close so she falls next to me on the couch.

"You didn't drag me into anything. I volunteered to be a part of all of tonight. And I don't regret it."

I tuck a strand of her dark hair over her ear, my heart thumping a bit harder. "You don't regret the madness you've been sucked into?"

She shakes her head. "Madness is my middle name."

I take a deep breath. "I'm glad the Ellison brothers haven't scared you away."

"I assure you, I'm not easily spooked."

"So . . . can we put this all behind us?" I offer, since

surely that's the only way I can manage to keep up the status quo with Elise.

"We can put it behind us." She takes a beat, fixing me with an intense stare. "But what if I told you I didn't think his suggestion was absurd?"

# 18

## ELISE

I should be shocked at the certainty in my bones. But I'm strangely not surprised at all that his brother's suggestion felt like the most right and true idea I've heard in ages.

Because I'm mad. I'm brimming with righteous anger for his brother. For the most underhanded cards ever dealt to a man. I can't let that woman—and I wouldn't know her from Eve—win by preying on Erik's love for her.

I set my hand on Christian's thigh. "I want to help you. I want to help you and Erik."

He drags a hand through his hair, his eyes registering surprise. He swallows and quietly asks, "You do?"

"Yes. Do you want to help your brother?"

He gives me an incredulous look. "Of course I do. But there has to be another way around it."

Perhaps I was wrong. Perhaps I read his nerves incorrectly. The last thing I want is to push this on him, simply because my moral compass is hugely offended by Jandy's double cross, which poor Erik never saw coming. I know what that's like—being blindsided by someone you thought would love you and only you forever. And this is my opportunity to save Erik from some of the pain I went through.

"Then, by all means, I'm sure you'll find it, and you won't have to resort to this way around."

He grabs my hand. "I'm not saying it would be a terrible solution. That's not what I mean."

"What do you mean?" I ask evenly.

*Don't get emotional, Elise. This isn't your battle.*

Besides, this isn't an emotional decision for me. It's a practical one. At the tea salon, I didn't think it was wise to accept his offer of help with the account, but now I can see we both would benefit from a revision to our arrangement. The truth is I'd love his insight on the travel industry, and I suspect he'd love to help his brother stave off this Machiavellian machination.

He sighs heavily and sinks back into the couch cushion. "I can't do that to you. After everything you went through with your ex-husband, how can I possibly put you through the ringer like that?"

I roll my eyes, the newfound strength flowing through my veins like a surging river. "You wouldn't be putting me through anything. This isn't the same. This isn't Eduardo trying to hoodwink me. This is you and me being honest and doing something that's right. Doing something that matters for your brother, and for you." As I voice the words, it hits me that this isn't only practical. This *is* emotional. But it's the good kind, the kind that brings a whole new round of closure. They're right and honest emotions, born from a chance to settle the score on behalf of someone who needs it. "You said you wanted to repay your brother for how he helped you onto the right path when you were younger. This is your opportunity."

"But what about you? What do you get out of it?"

I shimmy my shoulders. "I do believe there was a certain business expert who offered his help in nabbing a big travel account."

"I didn't think you wanted to mix business and pleasure?"

"Maybe now I do. I need a sharp mind. I need a fantastic analyst. And if you need something too, it won't feel like we're mixing business and pleasure so much as helping each other when we both need it."

"Elise, as much as I want to fix this shitstorm for Erik, I don't know if I can let you do this after what you've dealt with."

I scoff. "Let me do this? You can certainly say no, but this isn't about *letting* me. I'm not a delicate princess. I can handle this because I'm not interested in marriage. I'm not interested in forever. I am, however, ludicrously mad that someone's been taken advantage of. And it seems like you and I have the power to stop it."

He doesn't say anything, and I suspect he's taking a moment to process that I'm not messing around. "You'd really do this?"

"Not forever. But for a few months, for the time he needs, I would. I despise that she's been tricking him. I don't want her to get away with it. It's wrong."

I watch a range of emotions cross his eyes—eagerness, trepidation, and hunger for revenge. "Why do you want to right this wrong?"

"Because I can. I lost a few accounts when my marriage went south. It was awful, but I didn't lose my whole business. I'm rebuilding it. And here's your brother, completely blindsided by the love of his life breaking his heart and trying to steal the company your grandfather started more than fifty years ago. And you and I could tie the knot, and in that simple act, it would stop her."

He lets out a long breath. "Damn, you're fucking hot like this."

I laugh. "Oh, shut up. You're such a horndog."

"I know, but can you blame me? You're so fucking brilliant and beautiful and fierce, and your determination makes me want to fuck you even more."

I set a hand to his chest. "No talking of screwing right now. I'm talking about making a deal."

He shakes his head, as if chasing away the stray filthy thoughts. "Okay, deal talk." His eyes stray to his crotch. "Down, boy. We have other business right now."

I laugh at him.

He raises his face. "Okay, so where were we? You're going to do the absurd honor of saving my brother's sorry arse from his lovesick stupidity because you were burned by your jackass ex, and in return all I have to do is help you win an account? This hardly seems fair. Please, let's make it a condition that for every orgasm I get, I give you four."

I laugh so loudly, I'd be worried about waking up Erik, but I suspect he's dead to the sober world now. I lean in close, and nip Christian's earlobe. "That was *always* an unbreakable condition."

I pull back, and he wiggles his eyebrows. "Obviously. I was just testing you." He stares at me, as if he's trying to find the catch. "You mean this?'

"We've already made it clear that our existing relationship has terms and conditions. That means it also has an expiration date," I say, because what else could our arrangement mean? We so clinically laid out the details at the salon, and surely he wasn't expecting it to go on forever. No man wants that.

That's why it's odd when he blinks as I say those last words, as if that thought hadn't occurred to him. But quickly, he rights his course. "Of course, yes. We have an end date. Like a bottle of milk. Slap a best-by date on me, then chuck me in the bin." He finishes with a laugh.

Since he's laughing, I keep it light too—that's the best way to approach a deal like this. "Toss me there too, right?"

He nods confidently. "Both of us. When it's done, we'll be done."

"Exactly. But if it makes you uncomfortable, I'll find another business consultant and we can stick to the terms of our arrangement we discussed at the tea salon. I'm only offering this because we have the power to stop something utterly shitty."

"Oh, I'm quite comfortable with everything." He rakes his heated gaze over me. He cups my cheeks. "Do you have any idea how sexy you are?"

I laugh. "Your dick is quite distracting to you, isn't it?"

He yanks me closer. "You're distracting. You're going to ruin me."

Those words reverberate in my heart. I've already been ruined. Surely I can't ruin a man like him, and he can't damage a damaged woman like me. "I don't think that's possible," I whisper.

He shakes his head and murmurs as he loops his fingers through my hair. "You're going to ruin me, Elise," he repeats in a sexy rasp. "You're the sexiest woman I've ever known, and nothing in my life will ever be hotter than you wanting to save my family's business, all riled up, while you're dressed in that skirt and those heels, after I've had you coming on my hand at a tea salon."

His words light me up. They must ignite him too, because he tugs me closer, peppering kisses along my neck. "You're stunningly gorgeous and completely brilliant." His mouth slides down my throat. "And I want to marry you for three months, and I want to do everything to ensure you win that new account." His lips reach the tops of my breasts. "And I want to take down that cow who broke my brother's heart." He flicks his tongue against my skin, and I shiver as he raises his gaze once more, meeting my eyes. "And most importantly, I want you to come all over my face before I fuck you."

Heat sweeps through me like a fire, and I can barely take this closeness, this rampant desire in his eyes.

"Yes," I murmur since I can't form any other word right now. Everything with him is a yes.

He groans as he claims my mouth, planting a searing kiss on my lips. It's harder than he's kissed me before. It's possessive and demanding at the same time, as if he needs my lips bruised and bee-stung.

This is the first time we've kissed in private. We've kissed on the steps of the design show, outside the metro, and in the salon. But this is a kiss for behind closed doors. It's a kiss before clothes come off.

Yet I'm keenly aware his brother is in the next room.

He breaks the kiss. "This is what you do to me," he says, taking my hand and putting it between his thighs so I can feel his hard length.

He's beyond aroused. He's thick and hard and hot even through his jeans, and I want to climb on top of him, slide down on him, and ride him right here on the couch in his living room.

Only we can't. "I'm not going to sleep with you for the first time when your brother's drunk in the other room."

"I know," he moans, and it sounds like sad resignation. "But I'm very patient, and I can wait for you."

"There are some things you don't have to wait for though," I say, and my gaze drifts to his balcony.

"You want to see the view?" His tone is curious.

A hint of a smile crosses my lips. "I want to see the view from my knees."

\* \* \*

"Let me get this straight," he says as we step onto his balcony on the fifth floor of his flat. Below us is a cobbled street. Across the way are gorgeous apartment buildings. "You're going to give me a blow job in exchange for me agreeing to let you marry me to save my brother's company?"

I look at him and flash my most wicked grin. "You are correct."

"That hardly seems fair."

I drag my nails down his shirt and cup his bulge. "It's only unfair if you're assuming that you're the only one getting pleasure from the blow job."

He groans obscenely. "You're perfectly fucking dirty."

"I wouldn't assume that until your cock is in my mouth."

"Christ," he mutters, his voice already husky and rough. He grabs a cushion from the chair on the balcony and sets it on the ground. I kneel on it as I work open his zipper, tug down his pants, and free him. His cock says hello, and it's my chance to murmur my appreciation. He's long, thick, and velvety steel to the touch. I wrap a hand around him, and he takes a sharp breath.

"Fuck, that feels better than it should."

"You should feel spectacular. That's the point of our arrangement. Isn't it?" My tone is firm, brooking no argument. I look up at him. He gazes down at me. Understanding passes between us. We are on the same page. We get orgasms and profits from this—nothing more, nothing less.

"Yes. Our deal is quite possibly my favorite I've ever struck."

I stroke him. "You look better than in your pictures. I like you right-side up and rock hard."

He laughs. It's cut short when I flick my tongue over

him. His sounds turn into heady groans as I draw him in, running my tongue along his shaft.

His groans intensify as I savor his cock with my mouth. He ropes his hands through my hair, curling his big palms over my head, and I open my throat for him. He tastes clean and dirty at the same time. But the good kind of dirty, born of lust. It's the scent of a man turned on—turned on because he's already pleased his woman.

It's the scent of desire.

He finds a rhythm, thrusting into my mouth as I wrap my lips tight around his length. I might look subservient to anyone watching—and anyone could watch if they peeked through their curtains across the avenue—but as I wrap my hands around his hips so I can grab his ass and pull him deeper, I'm keenly aware I have all the power.

And I need it terribly.

I need the power play. I need to make all the choices, to enter this deal with my eyes wide open.

Neither one of us believes in marriage, but we both believe in honesty, and in honest pleasure. Giving it, rather than giving away my heart.

And soon, as he rocks deeper into my mouth, nearly robbing me of my breath, I'm awash in pleasure too. I am in its throes, completely gripped by it, loving this almost as much as he is.

He grunts that he's coming, and I dig my nails in tighter, and make sure I drink down every last drop that he gives me.

The sounds he makes are so intoxicating that I'm aching for him when he finishes and pulls me up. He kisses me madly, his hand slinking under my skirt once more, his groans guttural and wickedly thrilled when he finds I'm slick and hot.

"My turn," he says, and a minute later, his fingers are inside me, and I'm coming again.

Somehow, we've just sealed a marriage deal. Our agreement is to help each other in business, and to bring each other bliss.

Just so there are no misunderstandings, I wrap my arms around his neck. "This is a deal. It's an arrangement."

"We're in agreement."

"It has a beginning," I say, my eyes never straying from his.

"It does."

"And it has an end," I say, keeping my tone strong. *Resolved.*

I am resolved.

He nods, his expression steadfast. "It has an end."

# 19

## ELISE

"So this is how it goes."

My brow knits as I stare at Veronica across the counter at The Sweet Life, her flagship candy shop in Montmartre. "How what goes?"

"The process. The descent into madness." She grabs her phone, taps on the screen, then holds it to her mouth. "Dear diary, today my friend Elise lost the cheese from her cracker. She came into my shop trying to convince me that marrying the man whose nudie shots have graced her phone for more than a year won't end in heartbreak."

I hold up a finger. "Correction. I came here for a cinnamon stick, to give you the scarf I picked up for you at Annalise and Charlie, since it matches your fantastic complexion, and to tell you about my new plan to win a very potentially lucrative ad deal with a luxury hotel chain. Not to convince you of anything."

"Lies we tell ourselves." She taps her purple spatula

against a tray of confections. The spatula matches her apron—white with violet polka dots.

I bend to catch a whiff of the delicious scent of sugar. It swirls in my nostrils, with afternotes of strawberry and milk chocolate.

"Want one?" she asks.

"Chocolate-covered strawberry is hard to resist."

She hands me the candied fruit, and I pop it in my mouth. After I chew, I finish the thought. "It's not a lie. It's a plan, and a damn good one."

"Do you really believe this marriage is just business?"

"What do you believe it is?"

"A recipe for you to fall for his hot Viking ass while you play house."

I scoff. "Veronica, don't you know me by now?"

"Yes. And that's why I worry about you."

"There's nothing to worry about. It's all under control. It all makes sense. It'll be fine."

"Famous last words."

Drumming my fingers on the counter, I attempt again to deflect. "How about that cinnamon stick?"

She hands me one, and I lick it, savoring the spicy, sweet heat.

"And you think you're a cinnamon stick," Veronica adds.

"I assure you, I'm not into licking myself."

Laughing, she points at me. "Don't try to sidestep the topic by making me laugh at your dirty bird side."

"You're a dirty bird too," I fire back.

"Be that as it may, my point is this—you think you're tough and fiery, but you're really . . ." She pauses, scanning the shelves of confectionery before she grabs a bag of gumdrops, shaking it in her fist. "You're a lemon gumdrop."

"Aren't they sour?"

"Exactly. People might think you're tough, but on the inside you're sweet and gooey."

"That's not a very pleasant image. Perhaps you don't deserve this scarf." I tug it from my bag and hug the ruby-red silk number close to my chest.

She drops the gumdrops and makes grabby hands. "Don't keep the accessory from me. But don't deny you have a soft inside either."

"Hardly."

She stretches a hand across the counter, grabbing my forearm, imploring me. "You think you're nails and stone since Eduardo, but you're still that woman who believes in love. I know you. I know you are."

I bristle at the suggestion, raising my chin. "Love is for other people."

"I love you like a lemon gumdrop, and I think what you're doing is noble and also dangerous as hell," she says, dropping her grip as she moves to rearrange bonbons under the display case.

"We laid out all the rules," I say, with a bit of urgency in my voice. I want her to know I can handle this.

"But don't you like him?"

"Of course I like him. That's why I want to help. We both gain something from this, and I enjoy his company. There are far worse ways to spend the next three months."

She arches a brow. "You *enjoy his company*? Can you be any more clinical?"

I sigh heavily. "It's true. I like being with him, and I want to help."

"And what happens when you start to like him beyond *enjoying his company*?" she asks, sketching air quotes.

"I'll stop that from happening."

"How do you stop it? Do you truly think you can stop yourself from falling?"

"Yes," I answer in a split second. I believe it because I have to believe it. Because it's the only way to live.

"Look, I'd like to buy into that too, but it's not my experience. I was falling for Lars the boat captain, and the thing that stopped me was that we don't live in the same country."

"And the thing that will stop Christian and me is an expiration date," I say, keeping my focus on the practical aspects of this decision.

"An expiration date isn't the same thing as the whole damn country of Germany being between you. Lars and I texted after I left Copenhagen. I thought I could put him behind me, but I couldn't, so we kept in touch. We tried to make plans, but we could never be free at the same time, so I had to let it go."

I smile, trying to make light of the complications she's outlined—complications I'll have to be wise about. "Have a scarf."

I hand her the silky snake of fabric, and she tosses it around her neck. She pouts saucily and juts out a hip in a pose.

"Lovely."

"In any case, my little lemon gumdrop, since you're going to do this anyway, all I will say is this—keep your eyes wide open. Be aware of all the potholes. There are booby traps literally everywhere. If you want to come out of this with your steel heart—cough, cough—intact, you need to have your guard up in a whole new way."

"Guard up. I'm on it."

"Oh, and take some lemon gumdrops. You'll need fortification." She winks and hands me the bag of candy. Her expression turns serious as she sets it in my palm. "And I'll be here when the expiration date passes. You know that, right?"

"I do."

"There is no expiration date on our friendship."

"It's non-perishable," I say with a smile, then I thank her and leave. As I wander up the block to my home, I pop in a gumdrop. It's tart at first, as promised, but then it's all soft and sweet.

As if it'll melt into you.

Surely I'm no lemon gumdrop with Christian. I'll be a fiery cinnamon stick. Even though, as I open the gate to my home, delighting in the blaze of yellow tulips, I wonder if he likes candy that's a little bit tart at first but then sweetens as you savor it.

# 20

# CHRISTIAN

"I can't believe I lost the bet."

Griffin and I walk along the river at the end of the next day, the afternoon sun casting sparks of light along the water.

"Did we have a bet?"

"Yes," he says indignantly. "How could you forget?"

"What was it?" I bite into the egg crepe that I picked up at my favorite crepe dealer, wracking my brain to figure out what we wagered on.

"It was ages ago. But I bet a pint you'd be single until the end of time."

Laughing, I shake my head. "Sounds like some stupid shit we said at the pub, mate."

"That sounds like everything we say at the pub."

"True."

"Still, I'm kicking myself for losing the bet. It's making me laugh—the idea of you being married."

"I was married before. You're aware of that?"

"I know, but you're not now."

"So is half the population of the once-married people. Half of marriages end."

"I'm aware, but the amusement level on this is still quite high," he says with a smirk, as a twilight boat tour cruises by, kicking up a spray of water not far from us.

"So, me getting married makes you laugh. Thanks."

He waves a hand. "No. It's the bonkers idea that this will somehow be all business for you."

"Business and pleasure," I add, taking another bite.

"Need I remind you of the time you got involved with the client who wanted to enlist you as her boy toy and claimed she was knocked up, practically chasing you back to the homeland? At which point you swore off entanglements of that sort?"

"She was not pregnant," I add.

"She definitely was not, but back then you said not to mix business with pleasure."

"Elise isn't a client. This isn't exactly mixing the two. It's uniting the two for mutual goals," I say, explaining as clearly as I can how the deal with Elise is vastly different.

"That's hilarious, mate. How you say that as if you believe it."

I stop in my tracks and fix him with a serious stare. "I do believe it."

"Fine, fine. Keep telling yourself that. Just do me one favor?"

"Yeah?"

"Don't crush her heart."

"I don't plan on it, but I didn't realize you cared so deeply about her."

"Of course I care. Your girl is friends with mine. If

you break Elise's heart, Joy will kill you, and then my woman will be in jail for murder."

"And you've never had a thing for conjugal visits behind bars?"

"Exactly. Nor do I want Joy going to prison for strangling you. All you have to do is be a gentleman and don't hurt Elise."

"It warms my heart that your consideration is for me and for Elise, rather than whether you can dip your wick from behind bars or not."

"I think of everyone."

"Listen, it's going to be fine. I know Elise," I say, since the one thing I'm sure of is that she's even less of a fan of forevers than I am. "She has walls like I've never seen before. You think I have guardrails? I have nothing compared to her, and there's no sledgehammer on heaven or on earth that will knock down her walls."

"Good—keep it that way. You're all better off as is."

I hold up my free hand in surrender as I dive into another hunk of the crepe. "Look, if anyone's heart is going to be broken, it will be mine."

Griffin laughs. "Somehow, I don't think that can happen."

As I make my way home to check how Erik is doing, I hope Griffin's right. I can't deny there's a part of me that's the slightest bit nervous, and a little bit hopeful too, when I think about talking to Elise this evening.

That's when we'll finalize the plans for our wedding.

*Our wedding.*

## 21

**ELISE**

*Two and a half years ago . . .*

*Stop and Smell the Days blog*

*May 15th: One fine iris and lavender afternoon that I'll always remember*

My lovelies . . .

We don't wear perfume for men, do we? Not us *scentsual* women. We wear it because we are inexorably drawn to it. It is the signature of a woman. It's an invisible allure she leaves behind, a note held long and lasting that can turn heads and leave men wondering who she is, and what her story is.

And you've chosen that "note" for my big day.

I'd dreamed of this day for years.

Don't laugh. I'm like any girl in this regard. I've dreamed of white and flowers and sunshine. I imagined the warmth beating down on my bare arms and the fresh, clean smell of a garden that I walked through to meet my groom.

I was the girl who grew up in the city, surrounded by steel and concrete. That's why flowers whispered to me from Central Park, inviting me to play. Flowers became the antidote to my overwhelming, gritty city life. I went to the park and climbed the statues and pretended to carry a bouquet of violets and tulips across a field on my wedding day.

Then, I knew nothing of romantic love, or of sex appeal, of course. Now I do, and I want to share the story of my wedding day with you.

I slipped into a white scoop-neck dress, clipped my hair up on both sides in silver barrettes, and headed down the stairs of the inn in Provence, surrounded by family.

Once outside, my father walked me down the aisle—a flagstone path in a garden. This was a small, intimate wedding amongst the lavender bushes and vineyards. My groom's brother, his only family, stood by his side.

And I wore what you, my readers, my scentsual women, chose for me in the vote last week.

Marchesa Parfum d'Extase.

You picked it for me for my wedding day, and you

chose well. It's delicate and fresh with soft iris notes and hints of violet leaves, then a trail of night jasmine in its wake.

Now, a month later, as my husband is off traveling and I glance at the calendar, counting the days until I'll see him again, I open the elegant crystal bottle and I'm transported instantly to that day, surrounded by lavender and promises of always.

Thank you for the gift.


Yours in noses,
A Scentsual Woman

# 22

## ELISE

*Present day*

France won't do. There's a four-week wait. England adheres to some of the same rules. But Denmark? Blessed Denmark. You don't have to wait long at all to tie the knot in Denmark.

Christian left Paris last weekend, shortly after the bombshell news, and took his brother back to Copenhagen, since Erik couldn't bear to be in the same city as Jandy. That means I haven't seen Christian since the night at his place, but we've filed the paperwork, and he made a few phone calls to people he knows to push it along.

Here I am, stepping off the plane at the Copenhagen airport ten days later. I head through the terminal and pass security to find him waiting for me with a huge smile.

I'm hit with the strangest sensation when I see him

—I've missed him. I drop my bag, rise up on my tiptoes, and kiss him.

He hums against my lips as he kisses me back. An airport kiss. A reunion kiss. And it's so good it feels like it was worth the days apart, even though we didn't deliberately plan for this to feel like we're coming back together.

When we separate, he glances at my luggage. "Can I carry your bag?"

I packed light for the short trip, and I hand it to him. But I'd let him carry it even if it were heavy.

When we stride out of the airport, a sleek black town car waits for us. The chauffeur hops out, and says something to Christian in Danish, and hearing Christian respond in his native tongue as they toss my bag into the trunk is like pulling open the blinds on a darkened window. I've never heard him speak Danish before.

Inside the car, the driver turns around and raises his cap, nodding at me. His jowly face breaks into a smile. "Good afternoon, Ms. Durand."

"Good afternoon," I reply in English.

He returns his focus to the wheel, and I stare at Christian with wide eyes.

"What?"

"It's funny to hear you speak Danish."

"Why's that?"

"It's so different from French or English."

He laughs. "It's all consonants and Swedish Chef up-and-down rhythms, right? Funny sounding, isn't it?"

I smirk but say nothing. Because he's right. It's a funny language. It's not sensual like French or Italian.

It's clunkier, strangely childish in its intonations, and a bit odd to a woman used to the Romance languages.

"Admit it," he says then digs a few knuckles into my side playfully.

I laugh as he tickles me lightly. "I admit nothing."

"You'll admit everything." He dives in with both hands as the car swerves out of the terminal. He's a ferocious tickler, his fingers digging into my waist, and I gasp for breath as laughter sweeps over me. "You think I sound like a Muppet."

"I don't," I blurt out.

"You do."

"I swear," I say between harsh breaths as I wiggle.

"Tell the truth, Durand." His voice is firm, like an attorney in a film, demanding an answer from a hostile witness.

"Never."

More tickles rain down on me, and he brings his mouth to my ear and whispers something I don't understand a word of. It's ridiculous and sounds like "smorgen borgen."

I can't stop laughing, and I grab his forearms to get him to stop, but he's strong and determined.

And merciful too, I learn, when he lets up and laughs. He shouts something to the driver, and the man up front joins in, chuckling too.

"What did you say to him?"

Christian sets a hand on his belly and seems to do his best to rein in his own laughter. "I told him about a shortcut to my house."

I tilt my head to the side. "And that made him laugh?"

"I told him you were eager to make me an honest man, and that's why we needed to get there quickly."

"You're terrible," I chide, and then grab his shirt collar and stare at him sharply. "And what did you say to me a few seconds ago?"

He dips his face near my neck and maps my throat with feather-light kisses. "I said, *Wait till you try the lingonberry pancakes. They're delicious.*"

I swat his chest. "You are the worst."

"I know, but you deserved it for mocking me. You can make it up to me . . ." He slips from English to French. "By sucking my cock after the wedding."

His bluntness turns me on, and so does the fact that he made sure his dirty words were only for my ears and not the driver's. I thread a hand in his hair and yank him close, and we kiss the kind of kiss that's required after a filthy comment.

We break apart when the car slows, and we're in a residential area now. He takes my hand and clasps our fingers together tightly.

"Are you sure you don't want to stay at a hotel?"

"Is your brother at your house?"

He shakes his head. "He had to go to London on business."

"I'm completely fine with your house. The hotel seems silly." Once more, I wonder why he's concerned about my comfort at his home, then it hits me. I tense, my shoulders tightening. "Would you rather we stay at a hotel?"

"Why do you ask?"

"Since you've asked me a few times."

"I want you to be comfortable."

"Are you worried that letting me into your home implies a certain level of intimacy?"

He cocks a brow. "What?"

I don't mince words. "Is your home one of those places that's just for you? Not for a woman? Something that feels completely yours, and you don't want to invite someone in?"

He scoffs. "You honestly think after you've been to my flat in Paris that I wouldn't want you in my home here?"

"You've asked me a few times if I wanted to stay in a hotel. Yes, I thought that might be the case."

"My little mermaid," he says softly, "I didn't think *you'd* want that kind of intimacy. That's why I offered the hotel."

It's my turn to scoff. "I can handle the intimacy of seeing your toothbrush and forks."

He runs the backs of his fingers over my cheek. "I just want to make sure I'm not crossing your lines."

I roll my eyes. "We've already established the rules of the new road."

"And I aim to follow them," he says then recaps the parameters we discussed on the phone the other night. "We won't live together. We'll see each other more frequently than once a week. But not so much that seeing each other feels like an obligation."

"Seeing each other should feel like a pleasure," I add.

"Oh, it will."

"And photos. We'll take a few photos, so everything looks real on social media."

"Preferably photos of you in lingerie?" He arches an eyebrow.

"Oh, shut up. When I take *those* shots, they'll be for you only."

I silence the silliness of this conversation with another kiss. Because that we do without any concerns.

* * *

He's as handsome as he was the night I met him. More so because he's wearing a suit, and this man was made for suits. He stands in his living room, drinking a glass of water, flipping through a magazine as I emerge from the bedroom.

"Ready or not," I say, my heart skittering around like a wild bird. I set a hand on my chest to try to quell the nerves.

"Wow," he breathes out, his eyes exploring my body even though he's seen me so many times. Today I'm wearing a seashell-pink dress that hits at the knees. I decided white was silly. Perfume too. I didn't bring any.

My stomach flips as he admires me while putting down the glass and magazine. "It's not that fancy."

"I don't give a fuck if it's fancy. Your legs are spectacular, and you look so sexy in that dress and those glasses."

I raise my hands to my eyeglasses, adjusting them, though I don't need to. I'm fidgeting. He walks over to me, setting his hands on my nervous ones. "Are you okay?"

"Yes," I say, but the word comes out airy, empty.

He tucks a finger under my chin, forcing me to meet

his gaze. "Are you sure? Do you want to back out? Just say the word."

I shake my head. "I'm not backing out."

"You can though," he says, but his tone is reluctant.

"Hey. I'm here. I'm not backing out. We're doing this."

He smiles widely. "Yeah? We're a couple of crazies, aren't we?"

"Are we?"

Laughing, he pulls me close. "It's crazy."

"But brilliant."

"It's bloody brilliant. You know what else will be brilliant?"

"What?"

"Finally getting you naked and under me tonight."

"You're assuming I'll put out since it's our wedding night, are you?"

"Hope springs eternal. So does my cock when I look at you."

And once more, he disarms me with his charm. "I guess we'll see if the husband can get his wife into the marriage bed."

I press a kiss to his cheek. He turns and catches it on his lips, and it rockets into a searing kiss. But I stop it before it becomes hot and heavy. Not because I don't want hot and heavy, but because I haven't slept with him yet.

But the funny thing is, I'm sort of glad it worked out that way. I'm not trying to make this arrangement with him feel different than my marriage, but there's a part of me that likes how different it is. Eduardo and I slept together the first night we met. I've known Christian for more than a month and he hasn't been inside my body yet.

Somehow, that seems like the way it should be for us.

We leave, and I stop in the doorway, smacking my forehead. "We don't have rings. How could we have forgotten rings?"

He wiggles his eyebrows. "I've got it covered."

*  *  *

Inside Copenhagen City Hall, the wedding office smells like newspaper and efficiency as Christian Ellison promises in front of the officiant to love me. But the little quirk in Christian's lips says my husband's in on the joke. Only this time the joke isn't on me. We're both the comedians and the conductors of this love charade, and it isn't to hurt anyone or trick an innocent party, but rather to right a wrong.

It's a joke we're sharing.

But when his eyes lock with mine, he says without a trace of humor or teasing, "I do."

His words are weighty, and they hang in the air with import. For a fraction of a second, they feel honest, and my heart speeds up.

The officiant asks if I take Christian to be my husband.

"I do." I've voiced those words in the past, but in this moment, I feel the shackles of the first time I said them lifting off me. "I do."

Christian chuckles. "I do again too."

He reaches into his pocket, takes out the rings, I

presume, and holds open his palm. "A wedding gift from Erik."

The bands are platinum and unassuming, but gorgeous in their simplicity. He holds mine up so I can see what's engraved. The simplest words.

*Thank you.*

His says the same.

We exchange the rings, and the officiant declares us husband and wife.

That's it. Our ceremony took all of five minutes, maybe less, and yet it feels more real than my lavender one in the vineyard.

We sign the final paperwork and leave city hall legally wed, with the man in the charcoal suit poised to take control of his grandfather's company so that his brother's soon-to-be-ex-wife can't get her slimy paws on it.

A gift to his brother indeed.

As Christian holds open the door, I'm keenly aware that I don't want this union to feel less than the marriage of mine that was truly false.

Because in some ways—no, in nearly every way—it already feels like more of a marriage than the one I had before. It's an honest, open one.

On the steps, under a clear blue sky, with a view of Tivoli Gardens across the street, I grab my husband by the tie. "Do you want to kiss the bride?"

His blue eyes hook into mine, heat flashing across his irises. "So incredibly much."

I'm nervous, my fingers shaking, as I loop my hands around his neck. My heart stutters.

Even if marriage is a sham, even if *this* marriage is a

sham, my emotions right now are anything but. They rise in me, climbing my throat, fighting to escape. They're unexpectedly real and true, filling me with want and perhaps that hope I felt so long ago when I played in the park as a girl and imagined this day.

This isn't what I pictured at all.

But somehow, it feels like exactly what I need.

Christian seals his mouth to mine, and it's a soft and tender kiss. It's an exploration and a promise, and something about it is different from all his kisses that have come before. The gentle brush of his lips on mine makes me woozy. My knees go weak. He loops his arm tighter around my waist, tugging me close.

I'm the bride who's not in white, who wears no perfume, who is married for a deal the second time around.

But this kiss doesn't feel like it's part of a pact. It feels like it could become a new way of kissing.

When at last he stops, Christian looks dazed. "You smell fantastic."

"I'm not wearing anything."

"I guess it's the scent of you."

I suppose it is.

# 23

# ELISE

His mother engulfs me in a hug. "It is so good to finally meet you."

"And it is a delight to meet you," I say, enjoying that we don't have to pretend for his family—his mother knows the score. Even so, my brain lingers on one word. *Finally.* Everything has happened so lickety-split, I don't know why his mother would feel like we're *finally* meeting.

The three of us take seats at the outdoor café that overlooks the harbor, and we order a round of champagne. She clasps her hands under her chin and fixes a steely blue-eyed gaze on her son. Her cheekbones are carved, and I can see where Christian's blond good looks come from. "Tell me everything about the ceremony that you didn't let me attend this afternoon."

Christian rolls his eyes. "Because I'm sure you've been dreaming of watching me get married at city hall."

She swats his elbow. "I don't know why you didn't let me go."

He gives her a look.

I smile, loving the ribbing that they give each other, but especially loving that I get to witness it. I like that he's so open with his family, that his mom knows what we're up to. Mostly I love that he wanted me to meet her.

"It wasn't that kind of a ceremony." He looks across the table to me, his eyes holding mine for a beat that extends longer than I expect it to. "Besides, it was just between us."

My heart does something that feels like it's rolled over, flopped on its back, and put its legs in the air. Dog that it is, I tell that organ to sit up and focus.

"Be that as it may," she says, looking to me, "I am delighted to meet you, Elise. Now, tell me everything about the wedding."

I laugh, then give her the sparse details about our brief and perfunctory ceremony and show her the rings.

She sighs happily, shielding her eyes from the bright afternoon sun reflecting off the harbor. "Thank you for allowing me to experience it vicariously. He didn't let me go to his first wedding either."

I tilt my head, surprise hitting me hard. "You didn't?"

Christian shakes his head. "We were married in the United States. Vegas, baby, Vegas."

"You eloped," I say, as if the plot is thickening.

"Sort of," he says, laughing as he points at his mom. "Anyway, she gave me hell then. No need to do it again."

"That's my job. To give you hell." She snaps her gaze to me. "Although, I do hope you'll pick up the slack when I'm unable to give him hell. You have free rein to give him a hard time as much as you want."

"I appreciate the maternal blessing, and I will do my best to follow the directive," I say as the waitress arrives with three flutes of champagne.

His mother raises her glass, and we follow suit, clinking. "To the brilliant plan my sons hatched, and to the brilliant woman who's making it all possible." Her voice lowers. "My father—their grandfather—had the softest heart, but perhaps not always the most realistic expectations. I appreciate you making everything right for my Erik. I feel terrible for what happened to him."

"It's the least I can do," I say, and I'm glad this deal has been beneficial for both of us, or else I'd feel like some sort of martyr to the cause. But Christian has already prepped loads of business analysis and insight for my upcoming meeting with the travel client. His market analysis was spot-on and seems like something of a secret weapon.

"It's not nothing. It's everything." She glances at her son. "And maybe when you knock her up and have a baby, you'll at least let me come to the birth."

I nearly choke on my champagne. Bubbles shoot up my nose, tickling it, and a cough bursts from my throat.

"Mum, you're incorrigible," Christian chides.

"And where do you think *you* learned to be incorrigible from? The master." She smiles at me, a hint of wicked delight in her eyes. "Just teasing about the baby," she says playfully, then drops her voice to a whisper. "But not really. If he puts a baby in you, I'm not going to sit out the birth. I'll follow you around till you pop."

I laugh because there's nothing to say to that. There will be no baby, no popping, and no true mommy/daughter-in-law bonding. Even so, I think I love her already, and since she's been so blunt, I decide to assuage my own curiosity. "I have a question for you. Why did you say *finally* about meeting? Has Christian been telling you about me?"

"A year ago, he mentioned he'd met a woman on the boat tour and was very much looking forward to seeing her. And when he ran into you again at the garden bar, he called me and said, 'You're never going to believe it, Mum, but the little mermaid popped back into my life.'"

I rein in a grin as I make a check mark in a mental column of pros and cons about this man—*told his mother about me the night we met again*. Definite pro.

Christian slaps a hand on the table. "This conversation really ought to stop right now. The two of you are thoroughly embarrassing me."

I smile and laugh, meeting her gaze with the sort of look that says embarrassing him is what a mother and a daughter-in-law should do, and in this moment, we are indeed bonding. As I drink my champagne, I'm happier than I should be that he's introduced me to his mother.

I'm even happier that she's known about me from the start.

* * *

On the spectrum of things I've never expected, stepping into a marriage of convenience would be at the top of the list. Spending my wedding night at an amusement park would be a close second.

The spinner ride whips precariously high and my stomach rises in tandem, lodging in my esophagus. The giant gold eagle we ride in flips over, leaving us hanging upside down, high in the sky. I scream, a blood-curdling noise. The sound turns into a screech as the eagle rights us again, then sends us downward in a fast, wicked whoosh. One exhilarating, heart-pounding minute later, the ride slows, and soon, it crawls to a stop. The world is still wobbly, but the bar rattles loose and lifts up.

Christian sets his hand on my arm, steadying me as I stand, emerging from Aquila, the golden eagle ride at Tivoli Gardens. I grab my purse from the locker and slide on my glasses.

He rubs his ear. "You are loud, woman."

"So are you," I say, as the attendant opens the exit gate, and we pour out along with a few dozen other sky warriors who braved the thrill ride.

Christian, still wearing his suit but with his tie gone and stuffed into his pocket, shakes his head. "No, I wasn't. I was stoic and tough."

I laugh as we walk the pathway that weaves through this festive park in the heart of the city. "You practically squealed like a little girl the first time the eagle soared upside down."

He stares at me, his brow knitted. "Little girl? I think you're confusing me with someone else."

I pat his very firm bicep on his very strong arm and go along with him. "Yes, you're right, dear husband. It must have been someone less manly and less tough."

He smiles at me, mischief tap-dancing across his blue eyes. "Exactly." He bumps his shoulder against mine and whispers, "Hey."

That one syllable comes out sweetly, affectionately, and I add another pro in his column. That chart is weighted so heavily to one side, it's toppling over. I should find a con. It'll make the next three months easier. Not that I need to worry about that too much. It doesn't matter how many pros I find, this has an expiration date.

I am *resolved*.

"Hey to you," I say softly, then want to kick myself because that tone of voice won't help me find a negative in him either.

He raises a hand, adjusts an errant strand of my hair that was stuck in the arm of my glasses, and slides the offending lock over my ear. "Are you doing okay?"

"Are you going to keep asking me that for the next three months?"

"I might."

I stop, rise on my tiptoes, and kiss the corner of his lips. Oops. No luck finding a con there either.

"What's that for?" he asks.

"Just marking you."

"You want to pee on me next?"

"I might. Beware," I say in an over-the-top nefarious tone as we pass the gift shops that edge the small lake, making our way to the Ferris wheel.

"Elise," he says, his tone letting me know he's serious.

"Yes?"

"Earlier today, during the ceremony, did you think

about . . .?" His voice trails off as the unfinished question hovers like thick smoke.

"It's hard not to think about Eduardo. But mostly, I thought about how incredibly different this is because we've been so open about everything. What about you? Did you think about Emma?"

He doesn't answer right away. Instead, he scrubs a hand over his chin as if in deep thought as we reach the steps of the Ferris wheel. "I don't know if this makes me sound totally calloused, but I so rarely think about her." I pump a virtual fist because surely that's a con, that he doesn't even think about his first love. "Sometimes it feels like what happened between us was so long ago, it's like it was another lifetime."

"And you were a different person?"

He nods as he holds open the gate at the top of the steps for me. "I think I was in some ways."

The ride attendant says hello and gestures to one of the Ferris wheel cars. We go inside. "What's the biggest difference between the Christian of today and the twenty-one-year-old you? Besides nine years," I add, since I bet he'll go for some sort of age punchline. Could that be a con? Maybe he's not too serious about anything. Yes, that will definitely keep the chains up high around my heart if he's simply a shallow fellow.

He wiggles his eyebrows and punches his stomach. "Abs are still chiseled."

"I knew you were going to say something like that."

He loops his arm over my shoulders. "But they are. Chiseled."

I pat his belly. "Yes, and I like them. But I'd like you if your belly was soft."

"You would?"

I laugh and tap his temple. "I like the upstairs. That's what entertains me. So entertain me. Tell me something else."

And yes, there it is. I've found it. Christian is entertainment, pure and simple. He's fun and games. That's a pro, but in the end, it'll be a con when he can't take things seriously. When he can't take *me* seriously. And a good con, because it'll protect me. It'll keep the lemon gumdrop center of me from melting. Besides, peeling away his layers is wise. The more I know, the less likely I can be taken advantage of again. Knowledge is power.

"Tell me something I wouldn't recognize about you nine years ago," I add.

The car cranks loudly, making its first circle as he taps his chin. "I was more wound up then. Like I was turbo-charged and caffeinated."

I squint, trying to picture a manic Christian. "I can't see you that way at all." He has a relaxed ease about him. Perhaps that's because he's a true man of leisure. Young retirees can come and go as they please.

"I was like a coiled spring when I was twenty-one. I worked non-stop. I wanted so much. I think the fact that I'd had so little focus in uni for a while changed me. Once I had it, I was filled with the need to do things. To make money, to buy and sell, and keep flipping investments into bigger investments," he says, as the car whirs higher in the air then stops as more passengers get on below.

"And all that ambition played a part in your marriage not working out?"

He nods. "We didn't want the same things in life.

We didn't want the same things from the marriage. I suppose that's similar to what happened to you."

I scoff. "Safe to say we wanted *very* different things."

The car ascends to the top of the wheel, rising in the twilight sky above the top of the other rides. The panorama of the capital city comes into view—palaces and canals, and all the twinkling red, white, and green lights of the park below us.

"But really, the hardest part of my marriage not working out was reconciling that I wasn't like my father," Christian adds, and I jerk my gaze back to him. This is the first time he's mentioned his father.

"What do you mean?"

"He's been married and divorced three times. I think that's another reason my grandfather was so specific about marriage in the details of his company handover. He didn't want us to wind up like my dad, especially since Dad hurt my mum so much."

The picture of him fills in, details and angles becoming crisper and clearer, and another pro reminds me of its existence—the way Christian cares for his mom. Hell, the woman herself is a pro in the list; she's a doll, and I love her. "He was looking out for you, and for his daughter, in a way."

Christian nods as the ride circles low then rises once more. "He didn't like the way our dad treated our mum. He wanted to see us all happily together forever like he was. I think Erik got that from him." He hums, a sad little sound. "And look at us, all split up, just like dad. But it's for the best, for me at least. I'm completely content with my single life."

There.

That's it.

The big con.

He's married to his lifestyle, and that's exactly what I needed to know. And what I wanted to hear, in fact. It's better this way. Knowing he'll never fall in love makes it easier to enjoy the pure entertainment value of Christian Ellison. Who cares if he has so many pros? They won't ever amount to anything that can hurt me, since we'll never truly get close enough.

He grabs my hand. "And I'm pretty content with our arrangement so far. With one exception."

Oh. Perhaps there's an even bigger con. *A girl can hope.* "What's that?"

When we reach the top once more, the ride slows as it begins letting people off below us. "It's our wedding night and we're not screwing right now. Instead, we're talking about our previous marriages. That's backward."

I laugh. That is indeed a drawback, but it's easily rectified. "In our defense, screwing is an inevitability."

Sex with Christian sounds delicious, and a clear pro. In fact, it sounds so delicious, I'm pretty much done with the fun and games of Tivoli, especially since I know this marriage will be like this park—just fun and games, no matter how many times he's thoughtful and asks how I am.

As the Ferris wheel chugs down, I tug him close, and whisper, "Want to get out of here?"

He lets out a dirty groan. "It's all I want. To get you back to my house and show you exactly what a wedding night should be like."

We exit the ride and practically race past the

sparkling lights in the center of the park. This might not be the field of flowers I dreamed of as a little girl, and it's not the vineyard where my family toasted with Eduardo and his friend. Instead, I'm at an amusement park, with a husband who hardly asks anything of me, but the glittery setting is a fairy-tale land in its own strange, unexpected way.

Do fairy-tale heroines have hot sex?

Of course they do.

Especially if they get married to save the hero's brother's company.

A fresh urgency powers us as Christian takes my hand and guides me through the park. We have to weave through the carnival games to reach the closest exit, marching past a group of rowdy teens playing basketball.

They're having a blast, and I am too.

Until someone shouts *duck* and a basketball slams into the back of my head, knocking me down.

# 24

# CHRISTIAN

I open my palm. "Take these."

She pops the two Tylenol in her mouth and chases them with a glass of orange juice I give her.

"I'm shocked."

"By the horrific aim of drunk teens shooting basket-balls?" Wincing, she rubs the back of her head, settling farther into my couch. I brought her back to my place seconds after she crash-landed on her knees.

"I'm shocked at you. I had you down as the worst patient ever."

"See? I'm full of surprises. I love being doted on. Now, please cover my scrape with a Band-Aid," she says in a deliberately dainty tone, pointing to the tear on her knee. "Since you like being a nurse."

The funny thing is, I do like taking care of her. I like that I *was* the one to wrap an arm around her, shield her as we walked out of the park, and hail a cab faster than any man has ever hailed a cab in the history of men hailing cabs.

I head to the bathroom, grab a bandage, and return to her, so I can press it over the scraped-up bit of skin.

"Why did you think I'd be a terrible patient?"

"You're so stubborn I figured you'd be completely pig-headed about letting me take care of you."

"I guess you were wrong."

"I guess I was."

I smile to myself, but I don't tell her how much I like being wrong on this count.

When I'm done, I sit next to her. "Okay, so the head still hurts?"

"Yes, but it's getting better."

"And the knee smarts?"

"Definitely, but I'll live."

"Living is good. I recommend it. Does anything else hurt?"

She seems to consider the question, then taps her forehead. I lean to her and press a kiss to it. "Anything else?"

She hums as she runs her hand over her cheekbone.

I know where this is going, and I like it. I brush a kiss to her cheek next. "What else?"

She gestures to her lips and pouts. "This hurts a little."

"Let's see if I can make it better." I kiss her lips, and I'm rewarded with a soft, sweet sigh as her arms loop around me.

When I break the kiss, I meet her eyes. "So, you're all better?"

She shakes her head, affecting a shy little smile. "I realized there's one more thing that hurts."

"What's that?"

She taps the hollow of her throat and then drags her finger down to her breasts, and I groan. "Definitely, that needs a lot of TLC."

I dip my face to her neck, kiss her there, then travel down her chest to her cleavage. She wriggles against me and yanks me even closer. I kiss the tops of her breasts, and she gasps, arching her chest against me.

I look up. "Does that hurt a lot?"

"So much." She drags her hand down her belly to right below her waist. "And there. Definitely there."

I grin as my hands make their way to her back, and I find the zipper on her dress. I slide it down and make quick work of the rest of her clothes, till she's down to her white lace panties.

"Ah, you did wear white."

She smiles, then her smile disappears, and a flicker of nerves seem to pass over her brown eyes. "I wore them for you. I thought you'd like them."

*White. Wedding night.* It's almost too much to contemplate that this is where fate, or life, or circumstance has led us. That even though we agreed more than a week ago that we wanted each other's bodies, we haven't been able to have them till now.

I don't want to linger on the fact that I'm finally going to fuck her on our wedding night, but I can't deny that this moment feels like precisely the right time. Elise doesn't just excite me sexually. Her mind captivates me. Her quick wit, her big heart, and her blunt honesty are huge turn-ons. She's been turning me on since the day I met her, and tonight there will be no stopping me from showing her how much.

I wrap my fingers into the waistband of those perfect white lace panties. "I do like them," I say, in a rasp. "I like them so much, I want them gone."

I drag them down her legs, then feast my eyes on the gloriousness of her naked body. Smooth, creamy skin, perky breasts, and a landing strip that points to where I want to be.

"White was perfect," I add, as I cup her between her legs, then stroke her with my fingers.

She's soft and slick, and so fucking ready for anything and everything. She arches into my hand and whispers, "Kiss me."

I oblige, gladly moving down the couch and wedging my shoulders between her beautiful thighs. A sexy, greedy sigh falls from her lips, and she's already pushing my head to the center of her legs as she parts her thighs for me.

God, that move, right there. Watching her open for me. Watching the look in her eyes—want and need and maybe, just maybe, a touch of something more I can't define—sends sheer desire shooting down my spine.

The lust in her gaze, the vulnerability in her position—it's a gift. And it's one I'm so fucking grateful for.

A gentleman should always thank a lady for giving him the gift of her body. I'll thank her by lavishing attention on her with my tongue.

Pressing my hands to her thighs, I dust my lips against her skin, close but not quite all the way to her center. The smell of her makes me crazy; it turns me to steel. But as much as I want to devour her, I love the tease. I nip the flesh on her inner thigh, and she moans.

I nibble my way up, as she grabs and tries to pull

me to her. Smiling against her thighs, I bite again and whisper, "Soon, soon, my little mermaid."

"Now, now."

She's a magnificent beggar.

I switch to her other thigh, peppering more bites and nibbles along her flesh, then I rub my stubbled jaw along her center, and she arches her back and cries out, my name falling from her lips in a desperate pant.

I'm desperate too. Desperate to taste, touch, have.

I throw in the towel, and turn my face to her wetness, delivering a hungry kiss there.

She moves with me, matching every lick with an arch or a bow of her back, her hands curling tighter around my head. I'm as close as I can be, and I love being surrounded by the evidence of her bliss. She murmurs and moans as my tongue flicks faster. She lets her knees fall open wider, like she wants to spread them as far as she can.

She's so open, so surrendered, so completely unabashed in her sensuality. I can barely take it, and I swear I'm not just licking her. I crave her so damn much that I'm fucking her with my tongue, devouring her with my mouth. She cries out, arching her back high and shuddering as she comes on my lips, her taste flooding my tongue, her sexy scent filling my head.

She moans for ages, saying my name, panting wildly, and making incoherent sensual sounds that I want to bottle and listen to again and again. I could get addicted to the way she comes, how she lets go so completely. She makes me want to give her orgasms over and over—she makes me want to give her everything.

For a moment, that thought terrifies me. This should be just sex. I know that's all that we're having. But somewhere along the way, it's started to feel more than the physical. It's started to feel like something else entirely.

I need to shake off those thoughts. We have a deal, and sex is part of that deal.

I stand, strip off my shirt and trousers, and get down to nothing, reminding myself that just because she's easy to fall for, that doesn't mean it would be wise to let go.

She props herself on her elbows and stares at my cock. "Well, I think you'll be more fun to ride than the eagle."

Laughing, I say, "I should hope so."

"Hey, the eagle was a lot of fun."

"Then get on me and let's see how I compare." I flop beside her. We already had the safety talk and decided we could go bare, so she straddles me and positions herself over my length. She rubs her thumb along the head, sliding over a bead of liquid that she brings to her mouth. She sucks it off, closing her eyes, as if she's tasting the most delicious thing ever.

Holy fuck. I've seen nothing sexier in my whole life than my wife savoring me.

I blink away that word.

Elise.

Elise.

*Elise.*

But she's also my wife for the next three months, and that turns me on in some base, filthy, and wonderful way. "I want to fuck my wife."

"I want to fuck my husband," she says, just as fiercely.

My breath hisses as she takes me in hand and rubs me against her. I groan at the extraordinary feel, then I grunt loudly as she lowers herself onto my shaft, sending sparks of electricity through my body.

Sliding down, she takes me all the way. Pleasure ripples through me as she rises up. My gaze drifts to where we meet, and my dick throbs harder as I watch us, the way she takes me in, then how I slide nearly all the way out.

My hands grip her hips tightly as she rocks, taking her time at first, then finding a faster rhythm. I run my hands up and down her body, over her belly, cupping her breasts, memorizing her everywhere.

I settle a hand between her legs, my fingers stroking, and in seconds, she's shaking and shuddering on me. She falls forward, slamming her hands to my shoulders, her body trembling as she whispers savagely, "I'm coming."

I didn't need the heads-up. I could tell. But it's so erotic, so incredibly sexy to hear her say it unbidden, like the sensation is so intense she had to voice it, that I fuck up into her harder, thrusting faster. As she comes down from her high, I flip us, so she's on her back. I hike her legs over my shoulders and drive deep into her again.

She ropes her hands around my neck, urging me on. "Come with me."

I'm nearly there, and the thought that she might come again is nearly too much. "Can you? Come again?"

She nods. "I think so. Just keep doing that. Keep doing everything."

Her eyes don't stray from mine, and the connection between us is so intense, so electric. I'm not sure at all why, or where it's coming from, but it's wholly new and completely fantastic to feel this sort of ecstasy racing through every cell in my body.

Her eyes flutter closed, and her lips fall open, and her face turns into a picture of exquisite bliss as she trembles and lets out the neediest, sexiest moan I've ever heard, chasing it with a wild *yes, yes, yes.*

Whatever teasing, whatever fun and games have existed between us, are gone, and a raw, honest desire is all that's left. And it's all I need to join her. Her pleasure flips the final switch in me. I thrust deep and hard, coming inside my wife, the pleasure blotting out the warning sign in my head that tells me not to develop any feelings for her.

Correction—any *more* feelings.

"And that's how I envision Durand Media marketing the Luxe Hotel's new European resort locations."

The CEO, Nate Harper, leans back in his leather chair in the boardroom at his Place de la Madeleine offices, steepling his fingers. "Tell me, what do you see as the single biggest marketing challenge in entering the new marketplaces?"

I push up my glasses, and I answer with confidence. "The biggest challenge is also the biggest opportunity. It's reaching millennials, who will then become loyalists. But we need to connect with them first, and I'm prepared to," I say, detailing more of how my agency can reach that key market for his hotel.

He fires more questions, and for each one I have an answer. The market insight is spot on, he says, and I have my . . . *husband* to thank for that. A whiz, sharp with insight and concise with analysis, he provided exactly what I needed to complement the creative vision I have for this campaign.

At the end of the meeting, Nate rises and clasps my hand in a long, hearty shake. "Very impressive. We hope to make a final decision soon. Thank you so much for coming in, and I'm glad Armand made it possible for us to meet."

I beam. "I look forward to hearing from you."

I'm giddy as I leave his offices. I practically punch the sky once I'm a block away and can properly let all my excitement bubble over.

I grab my phone and sit on the steps of L'église de la Madeleine, the massive church that's the anchor of this section of the city. Briefly I contemplate texting Veronica or Joy, or maybe even my brother. But honestly, there's only one person I want to share this news with first.

The person who made it possible for me to go in there today and kick ass. I haven't seen Christian in ten days, not since the weekend we were married in Copenhagen. He left for London to meet with board members and a few key shareholders the day after our wedding. As the married one now, Christian's fronting the firm, but Erik is running it as he's always done. Once Jandy's shares are bought back in a few months, Christian and Erik will run the company as the majority shareholders, though Erik will still be the front man.

I do love their closeness and the way they depend on each other and trust each other unconditionally. Sometimes I wish I was closer to my brother, Jay. He looks out for me, and I know he cares for me deeply, and I love the little necklace gifts he gives me. But we don't have the sort of connection Christian and Erik have. Jay is busy with his life and his family over in New York, and I'm busy with my life here.

I click on my text messages, ready to type out a note, when I find Christian has already sent me one.

**Christian:** Tell me everything. Did you blow them away?

**Elise:** I think so. I feel like I nailed it.

I'm grinning crazily as the sun beats down, and passersby crisscross in front of me, parking themselves at tables and steps leading into the house of worship.

**Christian:** Excellent. I knew you would.

**Elise:** Your insight was amazing. I felt like a rock star, peppering off numbers and analysis. You are a god at that.

**Elise:** Oh, you're also a god in bed, but I think you know that already.

**Christian:** Why, yes, please do compliment me more. It feeds my ego and makes other parts larger too.

I laugh as I stare at the message, as if I'm in my own private flirty bubble right now, even as God and tourists peek over my shoulder.

**Elise:** I like everything about those other parts. And I like that quick brain that made this possible.

**Christian:** I'm glad I can be useful. But seriously, it was all you. You can only nail something if you know what to do with the info you were given. Now we need to celebrate.

*Celebrate.* That's one of my favorite words. Celebrations imply champagne, high heels, and nights out with friends. I've always loved a *celebration* because it means there is good news, and good news brings that most elusive of emotional states, one that's so hard to truly attain and sustain—happiness. But I feel it now, and I'm aware of how quickly it can disappear. Best to embrace moments like this.

**Elise:** How do you want to celebrate?

**Christian:** Ideally, by licking champagne off your breasts. But I think before we get to that, we should do something fun. What do you like to do for fun? Besides go on crazy roller-coaster rides, shop for your friends, plant flowers, and enjoy fancy and decadent meals out.

My heart does a little jig—he already knows some of the littlest details about me, like my penchant for showering my friends with gifts for no reason. Those are my favorite kind of gifts—pointless ones, because that's the point.

**Elise:** All of the above, and I also like dancing.

**Christian:** Swing? Tango? Foxtrot? Please say no as I can't do any of those, and ballet is out of the question.

An image flickers by of the type of dancing I want to do with Christian, and I wonder if he's any good at it.

**Elise:** None of the above. I mostly like dancing late at night in clubs when I can let loose with my girlfriends.

**Christian:** Do you want to go clubbing with your girlfriends, or do you want to go with me when I return this weekend?

I write back, the answer falling from my fingers so easily, so smoothly, that it feels like the only way possible I could want to celebrate, though I haven't yet won a thing.

Except, perhaps, a night out with the man who's front and center in my mind.

**Elise:** With you.

# 26

## ELISE

Saturday looms before me like the face of the clock, the second hand ticking obnoxiously in my ear.

I busy myself with work in the morning, cloistering myself in the office with Polly, my creative director, who's whipping through Photoshop mock-ups for the Luxe. Just a few extra items to send to Nate. Call it campaign Impress the Hell Out of Him.

As I look up from the media plan, she smiles, points to her screen, and declares, "Booyah."

It always makes me laugh when she blurts out supremely American sayings. She is American, but she also says them with a certain over-the-top flourish.

"And what has earned your *booyah* seal of approval?"

She slides the laptop in my direction, showing me a new concept for a social campaign. My eyes widen, and my marketing bones hum. "That is booyah and a home run."

She nods approvingly. "You haven't been away from

the homeland too long. You still know our little sayings."

"You know I can still shoot the breeze," I say, with a wink.

Polly has been with my agency for four years, and we've bonded over a love of marketing, and of being Americans working abroad. She flicks her pink-tipped blond hair off her shoulders and gives me an inquisitive look. "Also, I don't think I've said this, but you seem happier lately."

I blink, surprised at the forthright comment, but then she's always been like that. "I do?"

"There was a time when you weren't—" She shakes her head, as if she can't find the words. "I think for a while you put on a happy face and sort of made it through what I suspect was a tough time."

She doesn't know *all* the sordid details. At least, I don't think she does, and I could kiss her for phrasing her words more diplomatically than Dominic did.

"Now," she says, gesturing to me, "you seem to be glowing."

"Don't even say it. I'm *not* pregnant."

"I would never suggest that. I'm just glad that you seem so buoyant." Her eyes drift to my silvery wedding band.

I follow her gaze and nod. "I'm glad to hear that it's evident."

I don't elaborate, and she doesn't ask, and I like it that way. My new marital status isn't a secret, but it's not something I feel the need to announce to my employees.

For a moment, though, I wonder. I worry. If my

attention wandered during my whirlwind marriage to Eduardo and during the fallout too, what does it mean that Polly is able to read me now? Even though the situations are vastly different, is it good or bad that she can tell I'm in a better place emotionally? And does that mean I'm not giving my all to my work?

I try to reach for an answer, but none comes easily, so I decide being in a better place is a better thing, plain and simple. That *better place* is also synonymous with *here*—me at the office on a Saturday morning, pouring all my focus into work. I'm on the cusp of brand-new opportunities, rebuilding and shooting past the place where my agency was a few years ago. Maybe an arrangement where everything has been brokered from the start is the best kind for my bruised heart and my wounded business. Both are healing. Both are becoming stronger on the other side.

"Anyway, I like seeing you happier," she says as she shoulders her messenger bag.

She leaves, and I stay, finishing a few items and sending along a marketplace insight to Nate on Copenhagen, gleaned both from Christian's analysis and my own observations of the city during my trips there. Nate replies quickly: *That's interesting! I hadn't thought of those angles.*

A grin spreads across my face as I move the mouse to close down my inbox.

But a new message pops up before I shut down. It's from John Thompson, the head of the Thompson Group. He's probably vying for Nate's account.

*Hey Elise! How are you? Should we meet for drinks? Maybe we can join forces and discuss winning some deals together?*

I give his email the side-eye. He's a competitor. I don't want to meet with him to join forces, but I also believe in keeping your enemies close.

I reply: *I'm pretty busy, but my schedule should free up in a week or two. Talk then?*

He writes back swiftly: *Count on it.*

I take off soon after. I cut across the city to The Marais, where I spend the afternoon wandering through the intricate network of streets, the curvy jigsaw puzzle of one of the oldest parts of Paris, its cobbled passageways that cars can barely squeeze through. Some days, when I'm in the maze of The Marais, I feel like no one can find me. Like my phone is uncallable, my life untraceable. Like I'm one with the place.

Over the years, I've tried to truly understand my ties to this country, given I spent my first two and a half decades of life in New York. Sometimes, it's the creative heart of the city that I discover in unusual places. Like the whimsical cookware store I stroll past that sells antique rolling pins and irresistibly mismatched saucers and cups. I pop in and pick up a white rolling pin with red handles for Veronica.

Or the shop on the corner that still boasts an old sign reading "atelier" even though it peddles eclairs. The baker never removed the sign. I stop in and buy a small box of caramel eclairs for my next-door neighbor who doesn't get out much since her hip surgery but still craves her favorites.

I don't always find the answers to my questions about why I'm drawn here even when my family is still stateside, but Paris seems to be the true north on my compass. It points here.

As I turn the corner, I stumble across a café I've never been to before, with carnival music playing softly inside. It's parked right across from an eight-room hotel I've heard of—a decadent little inn said to have the most opulent rooms, complete with gold fireplaces and ornate decorations, like a celebration of debauchery.

Maybe that's why I like this city. If you want to celebrate, it's easy. Food, and wine, and drink, and treats are everywhere, and you never have to travel far to indulge.

I take a seat at an outside table and order coffee as I gaze at the hotel, remembering my first time in this city. I was six and Jay was twelve, and I felt like Madeline from the children's books. Maybe Fancy Nancy too.

For so long, I was raised out of place. I was the half-sie, as I joked with Christian. The child of French parents, speaking that language at home, embracing that culture behind closed doors, while to the outside world, I went to American schools and American classes and lived in an American city. All of that shaped me. It shaped my brother too. But the funny thing is he stayed behind, or maybe he stayed where he was always meant to be.

As for me, I was restless. I never felt truly content until I boarded a plane and spent my junior year of college here. That was the first time I felt the hummingbird beating in my heart slow to a more reasonable pace, one that didn't make me frantically wonder what was around the corner and if I'd fit in.

When I moved here, I felt distinctly like all my memories had come home, and all my new ones would be crafted inside the city walls. The city was like a calming hand on a shaking heart.

At last, a part of me that had been unsettled could find peace.

As I sip my coffee, I return to my conversation with Polly about happiness. My mind boomerangs farther back in time, to the trip to Copenhagen with Veronica. As we'd left, she talked about how happy she was after her night with the boat captain.

Briefly, I wonder if I'm happier now for the same reason Veronica was exuberant—because of a new man. Great sex can have a hell of a halo effect.

Best for me to be wise to that, aware of it.

I'm especially aware of the impact Christian has on me as I remember our last night together in Copenhagen. I see his parted lips, the ripple of his muscles as he moved in me, how his hair fell over his eyes when he collapsed on me.

As I gaze at the hotel, it gives me an idea. Hotels are made for nights of celebration, and for lovers. For arrangements. For part-time trysts.

I grab my phone. Christian must be on his way to Heathrow now.

**Elise:** Do you want me to get a hotel room for tonight?

He responds immediately.

**Christian:** Next time. Tonight, I'm going to take you to your home.

A pulse beats faster inside me, spreading from my chest, down my legs, transforming into something else, something far more dangerous, something I don't really know how to name. He's never been to my house before, and it feels thoroughly intimate to let him into the place where my empty bottle of Marchesa Parfum d'Extase sits, sterile and bleached but still alive. A statue in a mausoleum. But it's not Eduardo I'm clinging to with that bottle. It's the reminder to never make the same mistake again.

I settle the bill, call Joy and tell her she's needed immediately, and head to one of my favorite boutiques. When she arrives, her red hair thick and curly, I declare, "I need a new outfit for tonight. I'm going clubbing."

"Ooh la la." She shimmies her hips.

"I need something that will make a man eat out of the palm of my hand."

She gives me a do-tell look with her big green eyes. "Any particular man?"

"Hush. You know who it is."

By the dress racks, she leans in close and whispers, "Just say it. Just say his name."

"I don't know why you're egging me on like that."

She nudges me with her elbow. "You've got a thing for your husband, don't you?"

I shoot her a sharp stare. "Please. I just want to look sexy."

"Darling, you always look sexy, and you know it. You want to look extra special for him, don't you, because you haven't seen him in two weeks?"

My heart flutters, and all these sensations popping around inside me are starting to drive me crazy. To wind me up again.

I need something familiar. Something reliable. I understand how clothes make me feel. I know how shoes delight me.

"It's okay if you like him," Joy says softly as she flips through a display of pink, blue, and neon-green dresses, shaking her head at each one.

"I do like him. That isn't what this is about."

"Then what is it about?"

That's the problem. I don't know what this wild feeling is—this unclear emotion rattling around inside me. It's a language I don't understand.

But this burgundy wrap dress communicates in words I comprehend. The skirt hits mid-thigh. It says *take me, have me.* I buy it and wander around the streets with Joy, so very grateful that this city has brought me friendships like this.

Maybe that's why it feels like home.

Because of these people.

* * *

Later, when I'm at my house and freshly showered, I slip into a black lace bra and matching panties. As I check out my reflection, the flush in my cheeks, I understand one thing with the crystal clarity of a native language: I want Christian to want me with a raging fire.

Because that's how I feel for him. Like every bone inside me has been set aflame, and the heat is swallowing me whole.

Standing in front of the mirror, I snap a picture with my phone, and I send it to him.

**Elise:** Just for you.

He's probably just landed, or he's on his way to his flat before he meets me.

**Christian:** Preparing to rip that off you very soon.

\* \* \*

I walk to the club with a drum beating in my chest, with music pounding in my ears. Anticipation winds tight inside me, mingled with want, chased by need. I've missed Christian over the last two weeks. Missed him more than I expected to.

As I enter the club, threading my way through the bodies writhing and dancing, my eyes adjust to the low lights, my ears to the pulse of the techno rhythm. I catalog the sights and sounds, the press of people, the clink of glasses, the smell of liquor and cherries and sweat.

I order a vodka tonic and drink most of it down. Then, everything in front of me, all the things inside me, become static once more when I see him.

My brain sputters, and logic and reason slink away.

I don't understand a single thing anymore that isn't physical, that isn't elemental, that isn't this man I married and don't live with, and hardly share anything with.

But he's drawn to me.

He stalks across the darkened dance floor with such purpose, his eyes intense. He finds me at the bar and reaches for my drink, taking a swallow, then placing it down. No words are needed when he cups my cheeks and drops his mouth to mine, kissing me relentlessly.

We say nothing, and that's rare. All we do sometimes is talk.

When he breaks the kiss, he speaks. "You're stunning."

What he doesn't say reverberates between my ears.

He doesn't say *you look stunning*. No, he says *you are stunning*.

With him, I feel that way, inside and out, especially as he takes me out to the dance floor. Somehow, I manage to say in a dry husk of a voice, "So are you."

He pulls me close and grinds against me, his hard body making his intentions clear. The temperature in me rises into the stratosphere. I don't think we're dancing. It's foreplay in the middle of this low-lit club, with thumping music and beautiful bodies writhing and twisting and crawling around each other, with sweat and music and alcohol. Lights flicker in swaths, so we only see parts of each other. I make out the cut of his jaw, the wave of his hair, the strength of his forearms, visible thanks to his rolled-up cuffs.

He yanks me closer. I don't know how he finds any more space between us to fill, but he does, erasing any millimeter of distance.

I rub against his thigh. He grinds back. I tug him impossibly closer. He growls against my neck. My hands thread into his hair. His grab my ass, curling around me.

We might be the most indecent couple on the dance floor, and we are swimming in a sea of indecency. Out of the corner of my eye, I notice a black-haired woman wearing a top that's falling so low I can see her nipples. She dances with her partner. Her lips are parted, and it's like she's on the cusp of an orgasm. I flick my gaze to the other side, and two men grind against each other, heads thrown back. Even though I can't hear their sounds above the music, I can tell from their lips they'll be escaping any second to finish off.

I stare at Christian. "I think everyone here is about to fuck."

He runs his hand up the back of my neck and tugs my hair. Not hard, but hard enough to send a shudder through me. "Yes. Everyone is."

He slams his mouth to mine and kisses me hard once more. Like I belong to him. In this moment, I do.

In a flash, we're gone.

He was right. I don't want to go to a hotel. All I want is to take him back to my house, even though it scares me, even though it feels far too intimate.

But my body has taken over for my head and my heart. Everything else has the night off except my libido, a dark and dirty thing that's making all my decisions.

We tumble out of the cab, and I open the green door that leads into the courtyard. His hands are all over me. He's touching me everywhere: my waist, my breasts, my hair. He can't seem to stop. His lips travel across the back of my neck, and I can't walk straight when he does that. I'm buzzing all over. I'm drunk on him, and yet I want to have another vodka tonic. I want to be his vodka tonic and to have him drink all of me.

As soon as we're inside, my purse and my keys and my phone spill to the floor. Our hands rip at each other's clothes, undoing buttons, tugging at zippers.

I yank his shirt out of his jeans, and he brings down my panties, saying, "I thought about you all week long. It kills me to go this long without being inside you."

I swallow, nodding. I don't know how we reached this point. I don't know how we became too desperate, too frenzied that we're about to fuck against my door. All I know is that's who we are.

I push his boxer briefs down his hips and his hard length springs free. I wrap a hand around him, thrilling at how hot he feels. Hotter than the last time, and somehow, hungrier too.

He groans. "I don't know if there are words to describe how much I need to be inside you right now."

"Don't describe it. Show me."

In one sharp, hot thrust, he's inside. The sound I make is carnal. I might groan for days. It feels spectacular, his hardness against my wetness. He yanks my leg, hooking it around his hip and driving into me. We go quickly, like horses at the race, tearing around the field, aiming for the finish line. His lips come down on my neck, his teeth connecting with my flesh, nipping and biting.

"Harder."

"My teeth or the way I'm fucking you?"

"Both," I pant.

He bites as he fucks, and I'm filled so completely by him that I'm nothing but feelings—delicious, intoxicating, ecstatic feelings. I'm all the glittering lights in Paris, all the thumping music in the club—I'm everyone's desire right now. I'm being fucked the way everyone else longed for.

I get to have that coveted feeling, to bathe in erotic bliss as this gorgeous, brilliant man consumes me against the door of my house.

*Consumed.*

The thing I fear most.

The thing I feel now.

The thing I want badly.

I'm consumed by his body inside mine, consumed by the way he wants me, and most of all, I'm consumed by my own profound longing for him, a longing that finds a wild sort of peace in this pleasure. I've avoided this, guarded against it, but now I'm giving in. I want to feel every single thing with Christian.

We twine around each other, all hot and twisting limbs. I feel a tightening in my belly coiling higher, until the pleasure bursts and I cry out.

He follows me there with rough, hard thrusts as my back slams against the door, as his noises drown out all the sounds in my head, and I know he's as lost in his climax as I am.

Sometime later, I blink open my eyes and we're still standing at my door, disheveled and sated, cheeks red, clothes askew. "Come to my bedroom."

He looks down at me and brushes a soft kiss to one eyelid, then the other, whispering *yes*.

Somehow that feels even more intimate than what we just did.

# 27

# CHRISTIAN

"Your bedroom is so girlie."

"It is, and I like it that way. Being a woman and all."

"Yes, I very much like that you're a woman," I say, and part of me wants to take her to her bed and smother her in kisses and tell her how much I've missed her these last two weeks. Still another wants to say, *"Holy fuck, what the hell did we just do against the door, because it's never been like that before. That intense. That electric. That . . . intimate. Was it that way for you too?"*

But me playing that role—the needy lover—isn't in our script. The casting breakdown for her part-time lover and temporary husband calls for me to keep her on her toes, entertain her, make her laugh, make her hot, and make her happy.

No more.

I survey her bedroom, checking out the white walls, the bright white comforter. Purple and silver pillows are piled high on the bed, giving it a feminine touch of color. Thin gauzy curtains hang down around the mattress. "This makes me feel like we're in Africa. Do you suffer from mosquitoes?"

She rolls her eyes as she wanders over to the bed and wraps her hand around a bedpost. She glances to the door. "You may go now."

I laugh. "Don't kick me out. My work isn't done."

"Well, I don't see how you could top door sex anyway."

I pretend to contemplate, tapping my jaw with my finger. "True. I better take off."

She pretends to show me the door, gesturing grandly to the exit. I make like I'm leaving, zipping up my jeans at last, but then I grab her waist and tickle her. Laughter bursts from her throat as I carry her to the bed, tossing her on it, still in her tangled dress. I pin her, my palms at her sides. "I'm staying. Admit it. You like me."

She looks up at me, her brown eyes wide. "Why does everyone say that?"

"Say what?"

"That I like you."

"Everyone says it?"

She nods against the mattress. "They act shocked that I do like you. All my girlfriends toss that out like it's some big surprise. Why would I date you, sleep with you, marry you for three months, if I didn't at least like you? If I disliked you, you can bet I wouldn't be doing any of this."

"Only if you liked hate-fucking me." I grind my pelvis against her. "Do you like hate-fucking?"

"I don't know. I suppose I could pretend I hate you, and we could see if I like it."

"New goals," I say, keeping it light since this is so much easier than telling her all the mad thoughts pinging around in my head. "But honestly, I don't really want you to hate me, even for the prospect of angry sex."

"You're very likable."

And see? That right there is another reminder to play it cool. I'm likable to her. I'm the fun guy. The man who won't get attached. That's why she said yes to playing my wife, and I need her to finish the show. We're only in the first act of a three-act play.

I glance over at her white bureau. There's a mirrored tray with a few charm necklaces—a Chrysler building, I think, and a Broadway sign. They're ringed by perfume bottles. "Didn't you write about perfume?" I ask, remembering that she had mentioned a blog at some point.

Her expression tightens, and she doesn't meet my eyes. "I still do. From time to time."

"What sorts of things do you say?"

She waves a hand airily. "This and that."

She's evasive, and that's not like her. I arch an eyebrow as I run a hand along her hip. I should be Mr. Carefree and Casual, but I don't want to let this topic go. "You don't want to talk about it?"

"Let's just say I put too much of myself in it, and I had to pull back. Make it more about the perfume and the scents."

I run my hand down her thigh. "Was it too much of your life?"

She nods. "It was."

"So why do it at all?"

She sighs deeply. "I haven't written a post in a while. I could shut it down, but I miss the camaraderie with my readers. I felt close to them, this random group of strangers who honestly weren't strangers. I met Joy through a perfume forum back when she lived in the States, and now she's one of my closest friends. But at the same time, I think pulling back, not writing as openly, was for the best. I feel safer."

"Does that make you happy? Safety?"

"Yes."

"Maybe that's why you're happy with me. I make you feel safe."

She shoots me a curious look. "What do you mean?"

"You've drawn your lines. I don't cross them. That makes you feel safe, and safety makes you feel happy."

She nibbles on one corner of her lips. "It's funny that you brought this up, because I was thinking about life, liberty, and the pursuit of happiness today."

"So American. And what did you think as you were musing on that?"

"I was remembering how my friend Veronica was going on and on about how incandescently happy she was after she banged this hot Danish boat captain in Copenhagen last year."

I laugh. "Banging hot Danish men with British accents should totally make you ecstatic."

"We should test this theory again. Just to be sure." She runs a hand down my arm, and her voice turns more serious, contemplative. "You do make me feel safe. I need that. Thank you for doing that."

A faraway look fills her eyes, and as I follow her gaze, I see her staring at the collection of bottles on her bureau. One of them is empty. My curiosity gets the better of me. "Why are you keeping that empty bottle?"

She closes her eyes and sighs, then rises, getting out of bed all rumpled and tousled. She walks to the bureau, plucks the crystal one, and takes it to the en suite bathroom. I lean near the edge of the bed so I can watch her through the open doorway. She drops it into the rubbish bin. It lands with a hard thud.

"Why did you do that?" I ask.

She stands in the doorway. "It was my wedding day perfume. I've needed to do that for a long time, Christian."

A pinch of jealousy flares in me and the feeling surprises me and pisses me off. How on earth could I be jealous of her dead husband?

But the vicious truth whispers in my ear. I'm envious in some terrible way that she's held on to him for so long.

She returns and sits next to me. "I needed to do that."

"You didn't have to do that for me," I say coolly.

"I did it for me." She tilts her head, takes my hand. "I don't love him."

I laugh lightly. "Good."

What I mean is *that's fucking great*.

"I want you to know that."

That's more than great. It's perfect, and I do my best to keep a stoic face while inside I'm pumping a fist in victory. I'm so fucking happy she's over him. This, right here, is the definition of happiness.

"Okay," I say calmly, since letting on how much this knowledge thrills me might push her away.

"I'm not holding on to him. I need you to know that. I held on to the bottle because it was a gift from my blog readers."

*Ohhhh.*

"The plot thickens," I say playfully, since her response makes precisely the kind of sense I want it to make. Selfishly, I like her explanation a lot—her past is well and truly her past. "You weren't ever holding on to something from him, then. You were holding on to something from people you miss having a connection with. You should reconnect with them."

"That's not a bad idea."

I grab her hand, looping my fingers through hers. Our rings touch. As I gaze at our joined hands, our metal connecting, I remember doing the same with Emma. Holding the hand of my first wife nine years ago, did I feel the same with her as I do in this moment?

I loved Emma. I don't question that. But did I feel like *this*? This sort of unexpected awareness of the way a person affects you, deep in your body, far into your mind?

I feel like I could talk to Elise about anything. I never had that with Emma.

"You do know I'm over Emma, right? It was years ago, but still. In case you were wondering." I need her to know there's no competition from the past—no ghost, no poignant memory. "I don't have baggage."

"You do seem remarkably baggage-free," she says with a smile. "But is being baggage-free your baggage?"

I shake my head. "If you're asking if I'm tied to my single lifestyle or have some über-commitment to being a playboy, I'm sure Griffin would say yes —"

"Why on earth would Griffin say yes?"

"Oh, I used to tell him my dream was to become a kept man of some gorgeous, brilliant older woman."

She smacks me. "You're terrible. Preying on older women."

I kiss her shoulder. "I can't resist them."

She raises an eyebrow. "Are you truly attracted to me because I'm four years older than you?"

"Umm . . ."

"Seriously?"

"No. That's not it, but I think you're fascinating. You intrigue me. I like that you're *not* focused on the same things a twenty-five-year-old is focused on. You're building a stellar international business, you're taking care of yourself, and you're looking out for friends. You have all this rich life experience, and yeah, I'd be lying if I said I didn't find it attractive. So sue me."

She pushes a hand against my chest. "Fine, then I like that you're younger than me."

"Oh yeah? You like boy toys?"

She scoffs. "Not in the least. I like it because it means you're more thoughtful."

"It does?"

She nods. "You're pretty damn thoughtful, Christian, and that's incredibly attractive."

I yank her closer. Maybe because of her compliments, possibly because we've moved past a wall, I say what I wanted to say a little while ago. "That was really intense against the door, wasn't it?"

She trembles. Like a muscle memory from sex moves through her. "It was crazy intense," she whispers. "We barely said a word to each other at the club."

"I think I sort of attacked you. In my defense, you sent that photo in your black lace, and I did give you fair warning."

She drags a hand down my shirt, unbuttoning it. "I liked being attacked like that. I liked the intensity of it."

"It wasn't too much for you?" I ask as she spreads open my shirt, and I push off the sleeves.

"I was wound up for you all day. As I walked around, I felt this tightening in my body, like a jack-in-the-box, wanting to see you."

Lust climbs up my legs, weaves through my chest as I undo the wrap on her dress, letting the fabric fall apart. "I felt it too. What is that all about? It was like a crazy drumbeat." I tap my chest. "Right here."

She nods, and there's a savage look in her eyes, a fierceness. "Once I saw you, it was like an explosion. Like we detonated. I don't think I've ever had sex that intense before."

The caveman in me thumps his fists. "I haven't either. But when I see you, Elise, I want to take you." I cup her jaw, holding her close. "I want to take you hard, and relentlessly, and I want to get so fucking close to you that you let go of everything."

She shivers. "When you fuck me like that, I feel consumed."

"Does that scare you?"

She nods. "But I don't want to stop it." She shoves

down my jeans and takes my length in her hand. I ache with desire, with this torrent of need that grows stronger each time I see her.

"So if I respect your boundaries and your walls, you'll let me keep fucking you like that? Like the world is on fire?"

Her eyes blaze with lust. "I do want to be consumed."

Something passes between us, something that feels deeper than the way I felt on our bizarre wedding night.

I know what it is for me. I know what it isn't for her.

And I know I have to keep a close watch on our arrangement, making sure I can make her feel safe while I also help her lose herself. Because that's what I see in her—I see a woman who wants so much, who craves so deeply, but who's terrified of what that hunger might do.

I suspect she wants to be the woman she was before. The one who wore her heart on her sleeve, wrote her bliss for the world, and shared herself with one person, believing she was the only one.

That part of her still lives, but she won't let it come out.

Maybe she will with me.

I move her against me, her back to my front, so we're side to side. I glide my hands around to her breasts, fondling them as I slide inside her easily. She moans, a low, sensual sound that vibrates between us. She leans her head back against me, her dark hair spilling over my shoulder. Her top leg hooks over my thigh, and she opens wider as I move inside.

It's that kind of slow, luxurious lovemaking session that feels like it could go all night long. As the minutes tick by and pleasure twines between us, my skin hot and slick against her and her breath coming harder and faster, I can feel her give herself to me.

This is the part of her she tries to extinguish. She's come out tonight, and she's surrendering to me, and it's fucking beautiful to feel.

It's not that our sex is particularly kinky or particularly rough. It's not that we're doing anything dirty or risqué. We're not screwing on the metro, or sneaking a quickie on the Pont des Arts, nor are we christening every surface in the house.

We're in her bed, which may be precisely why everything about this moment feels more intimate. I'm in a private place, belonging to a most private woman, and she wants me to pleasure her in a way that erases the world beyond the windows.

I don't need to blindfold or tie her up to do that. All I need is this white-hot desire that flows between us.

She turns her face toward me. I bring my lips to hers and kiss her as I move in and out. There is little that's artful about this kiss, but it feels like drowning, like falling under. I can't get enough of her lips, her taste, her breath.

She sighs against my mouth, and I swear it's as if her body melts into me. She's a liquid woman, all silvery-hot desire, and it wraps around me, making me hotter, making me harder.

And she takes freely. With no remorse, she soaks up all the bliss I want to give her in this luxurious, deca-dent indulgence. She comes once more, and it's a beautiful thing, the way her ecstasy moves over her body. She shudders and cries out, and it sounds like something inside her is breaking free.

When she comes down, she mumbles something about how it's my turn. I nip at her ear. "That would imply I'm done with you."

I flip her to her knees and push her down to her elbows. She turns around and watches me, and it's the most erotic, sensual thing to see her look at me like that. Pleasure rattles through my body, and it's mingled with all these new sensations, deeper emotions, and a fervent wish to make this arrangement last a little bit longer.

I bend closer, pulling her against me, covering her. She comes again, calling out incoherent words of rapture, and finally, I let go too, my world turning white hot and electric.

A few minutes later, we're sated and tangled together. She puts her hands on my chest and looks me in the eye. "Thank you."

I laugh. "Why are you thanking me?"

"For understanding what I need. For giving it to me. Even if I didn't know what I needed."

"I like giving you what you need. You should stop worrying so much about people wondering if you like me. I know the truth. I know you do."

"I do."

But that's the trouble. I have to keep it on *this* level. This *I like you* level. If I let loose the truth, I might lose her. I need her to feel safe with me, and safety means keeping myself at an arm's length.

The problem is I don't want an arm's length between us anymore.

I've fallen for the woman I made a deal with.

That's why I touched her like a starving man at the club, but this potent need didn't start tonight. It ignited when she proposed this arrangement. It took root when I saw what she'd be willing to do for me and for Erik. Marrying her in my hometown only sealed the deal, and all the emotions that raced through me that night in Copenhagen, the ones that seemed strange and foreign then, are crystal clear now.

The falling is complete. It's here. It's happened, and now I'm in love with the woman in my arms.

But this woman needs me to be the kind of man who doesn't fall so easily. And I need her to save my brother's hopes and dreams.

I segue to something else entirely as I press a soft kiss to her neck. "Mmm. You smell good. You should write about other smells you like. If you don't write about perfume, write about other scents."

"Maybe I will," she says, snuggling closer to me.

With her soft and malleable in my arms, it doesn't feel like there are any boundaries.

But there are. There most definitely are.

# 28

# ELISE

*Today . . .*

*Stop and Smell the Days blog*

*July 5: Apricot flowers*

My lovelies . . .

We must dispel a long-standing myth about tulips. There are some people who believe they aren't fragrant. Isn't that bananas? But we scentsual women know the truth.

Tulips are beguiling. They draw us in with their color, almost tricking us into thinking they won't overwhelm our noses. But once we lean in and inhale them, we know the truth. They are fragrant in their own way. The tulip wants you to get a little closer, to understand its soft honey notes, to uncover a hint of apricot. It's sweeter, softer, more floral, but with a touch of sex appeal.

That's the tulip for you. Don't let its pinwheel of colors seduce you into thinking it's a one-trick flower. It has so much more to it.

This morning, I snipped some from my garden, brought them into my sun-drenched kitchen, and filled a pewter pitcher with water. I set the tulips in it and thought of why I sought them out today in the first place.

That brought a warmth to my heart.

By the way, it's so nice to see you again. I've missed you all. I hope some of you can see me waving to you.


Yours in noses,
  A Scentsual Woman

# 29

# CHRISTIAN

In the morning, I find her in the kitchen, wearing a camisole and knickers. She's putting a plate of breakfast food together. There are no eggs in sight. "It looks great. Even without eggs."

"Oh, are you an eggs-or-bust person?"

"Eggs are everything."

She gestures to her purse, perched on her kitchen chair. "There's a market around the corner. Let me go get you some."

I step to her, cup her cheeks, and kiss her forehead. "No."

"But I don't mind."

"I don't mind going without. It's just eggs."

"It's only around the corner."

And I fall a little deeper because she wants to make me eggs. I'm so fucked. But if I let her get the eggs, I'll be fucked royally. Yep, I have to chicken scratch a line in the sand. My new border comes from chickens. "Fruit and bread is perfect," I tell her.

Over blueberries, a baguette, and a steaming cup of coffee, she takes out her iPad, a sheepish grin on her face. She taps on the screen then slides it over to me.

I read, and with each line about tulips, my grin grows. When I finish, I glance at the orange flowers on the table. "Happy?"

She nods, and there's almost a childlike glee in her smile. *I did this for her. I brought this feeling to her.* "Very much so."

After we eat, I help her clean up, then I nod to the door. "I should go."

I don't want to go. But I have to.

"Do you have to?"

My heart lurches toward her. I half wish she'd make this easier. The expiration date is so fucking far away, and I'm going to have to lie to her about how I feel for more than two months. "Don't you need to bury yourself in work today?"

She shakes her head. "No. Do you want to bury yourself in me today instead?"

Like I'm resisting that.

I throw in the towel, toss her over my shoulder, and carry her up the stairs, two steps at a time.

\* \* \*

Later that week, I meet her after work at a brasserie. We grab a table on the pavement, under the awning.

"Does this mean we're on a new schedule? Since it's not Friday or Saturday night?" I take a drink of my beer as a ragtag group of street violinists on the corner serenades us.

"Hmm. It seems we have graduated to a more multi-tiered arrangement."

"I knew I could wear you down."

Laughing, she raises her wineglass, and gives me flirty eyes over the rim. "Was that your plan when you flashed me your parts way back when?"

"Absolutely. I've been waging a war of attrition ever since you got the Christian Ellison full monty treatment."

She takes a drink of her wine. She hums as she sets it down, looking away, seemingly lost in thought. "Do you ever wonder what it would have been like if I'd found my way to The Jane?"

I take a swallow as I contemplate. "I've thought about that scenario many times. And I know the answer."

She arches a brow. "Do tell."

"We'd have had spectacular, wall-thumping sex that night, and I would've never seen you again."

"Why?"

I lean forward. "Because you weren't ready."

She laughs, but it's an awkward, uncomfortable sound. "I wasn't ready?"

I shake my head. "Not for me to unleash my brilliant wit, effervescent charm, or full suite of bedroom services."

"And how do you know I wasn't ready for the full Christian?"

"Because I had to wear you down a whole year later. That's how I know."

She raises her glass. "Well then, I really ought to drink to your persistence."

I wiggle an eyebrow and clink my bottle to her glass in a toast.

After a drink, she sets down her wine. "But I still think I might have given in sooner, rather than making you wait."

I scoff. "Doubtful. You loved every second of making me wait."

She grins. "Fine, let's pretend we met, had spectacular sex, and you courted me for a whole year in Paris. And the entire time I was secretly delighted with your pursuits."

"You were?" I like her story. I like it a lot.

"I was," she says with a smile, and I catalog this slice of an evening as yet another moment when I want to tell her how she makes me feel. But I don't. "And that will be our marriage cover story if anyone asks."

"It's a good story."

"So's the real one," she says, and she's making this harder by the second.

When we finish, she says she wants to head to a shopping street not far from where we are in Saint Vincent De Paul.

"Of course you want to shop."

She taps my shoulder. "I want to get something for your mother. What does she like? What is she passionate about?"

"Besides the prospect of grandchildren?"

She rolls her eyes. "First, a marriage of convenience. Next, she'll want grandchildren of convenience."

"If she could get them, she would. But truth be told, she likes egg cups."

Elise laughs. "That's where your love of eggs comes from."

I hold up my hands, shaking my head. "I have no need for egg cups. I just like the food."

Like she has a radar in her, she zigs and zags through the streets till she finds a store that sells, among other things, quirky little egg cups. She picks one that's blue with a chicken design, and later that evening back at her house, she wraps it up in sky-blue tissue paper with a silver bow. The finished product looks like something you would see in a department store, and my mother is going to love it.

I wish Elise wasn't such a perfect temporary wife.

"You're the perfect wife," I tease.

"Because I don't make demands?"

*Make demands. Shower me in them. I'll fulfill them all.* "You could make an occasional one. I'd be okay with that," I say with a wink.

"In that case, can I come see you play soccer?" she asks, using the American term for the sport I play.

"You want to watch me play?"

"I like you sweaty."

"I'll check the schedule and let you know when our next game is." I loop an arm around her waist. "And then you can get sweaty with me after."

"Obviously."

* * *

My translation work has slowed, but that's been deliberate. Once I stepped up to take over the transition of the firm, I couldn't spend too much time cherry-picking

Scandinavian businessmen and women to translate for. I've still nabbed the occasional plum gig—the kind I like best, where I'll translate for a dignitary or a celebrity.

Mostly, my work is here in the Paris office with Erik.

As I finish off a spate of contracts, Erik slouches into my office. He looks like hell. His jaw hangs open. "She . . ."

It's all he gets out.

"What is it? She what?"

"She found me where I was having lunch."

"Are you kidding me?"

He sinks down into a chair, his head falling into his hands. I walk around the desk and sit next to him. "What happened?"

He sighs heavily. "I was eating. All I wanted was to have a sandwich in peace at the café I like."

"The one she knows you like? The one she knows you go to?"

"Yes," he says in a sad and angry hiss. "She showed up, took the seat across from me, and asked if I'd be willing to talk."

"What did you say?" I ask nervously, because this hasn't been easy in the least for him, and because I worry about the firm.

He looks up, his blue eyes full of melancholy. "I didn't say anything, because I felt so fucking awful. I felt like I was still in love with her, and I hated feeling that way."

I swallow roughly, hurting for my brother. "I hate that you feel that way." I take a beat, then ask an important question. "What did she want?"

"She wanted to talk it out. Have a chat. She loves me, but she's not *in love* with me," he says, sketching air quotes.

I seethe. "That's such a cop-out."

"That's not all."

"What else?"

"She told me her sister is ill, and she doesn't have enough money for the medical treatment, and that's why she wanted to sell the firm."

I scoff. "Lillian is ill? That's a barking lie."

"What if it's true?"

I grip his shoulder. "Don't believe her. She lied to you."

He nods, his breath coming out shakily. "She tried to tell me it was the only way and couldn't I look into my heart to help? And I said I would have helped her if we were together. She could have come to me for help."

"What did she say?"

"She said she felt like she was always coming to me for help. That she needs to be able to do things on her own. That's why she left."

He winces, and I squeeze his shoulder again. "She's messing with you, Erik. You know that, right? This all seems incredibly dodgy."

"Does it?"

"Completely. Don't let her manipulate you."

His shoulders slump. "I don't know how this went pear-shaped. I don't know why I didn't see it coming. I had literally no fucking clue she would take a knife from the butcher block and stab the serrated edge into me. And that's how it feels now, Chris. That's how it fucking feels."

For a flash, I can hear Elise saying those same words. They sound precisely like how she must have felt when she learned of her husband's transgression. And in this moment, my anger, fueled by the short straw that two people I care about were handed, intensifies. I hate that they were duped.

Erik's voice breaks, but if tears were coming, he tamps them down, drawing a sharp and angry breath. "It's not right that you and Elise are putting on this whole production for me."

"I think I can manage pretending to like Elise a little bit," I deadpan. If he only knew the half of it—that I'm pretending not to be completely mad about her.

"Yeah? It's not so awful?"

"We're faking it fine, thank you very much. Enough about me. I want to know how I can help you. Do you still love her?"

He moans and shakes his head, then nods. "Yes, no. Yes, no. I want to be over her." He pushes out a strained laugh. "Can you get me a pill? Something, anything to make me not feel a thing for Jandy?"

I smile faintly. "If there were one, I'd get it. But in the meantime, want to go to the movies and see a stupid Will Ferrell comedy? Those always make you laugh."

He smiles, as if he can't help it. "*Talladega Nights*?" He places his hands together as if praying. "If there's a goddess, then some theater will be showing *Talladega Nights*."

"That theater is known as Netflix, I believe."

But there's also a theater in the second arrondissement where we find a Will Ferrell "retrospective" is underway, so I steal him from the office and take him to see Ricky Bobby tear up the racetrack.

If this isn't fate looking out for us, I don't know what it is.

* * *

When Friday arrives, Elise texts me to tell me she'll be at the field a few minutes before the game starts.

I write back that I'll see her when she arrives, and I'll kick a goal for her. I finish my stretches and look around once more.

A woman calls out my name. But the voice isn't the one I want to hear.

I look over to the edge of the field to see a tall woman with high cheekbones and dirty-blond hair.

"Christian, can we chat?"

It's my brother's wife.

# ELISE

My stomach flip-flops, and my hands are cold. I press the elevator button for the sixth floor, wishing I wasn't so nervous.

But this chance feels so big.

The Luxe isn't only a potential client. It's a potential client who could vault me to the next level. This is the goal I've been reaching for.

As I wait, my phone dings and a new note from John Thompson pops up on the screen. My nerves twist higher as I open it.

*Time to grab that drink? :)*

I close it. I don't want to be thinking of my competition when I walk into Nate Harper's office at his request. I do my best to sweep John from my mind.

The elevator arrives, and I step inside, shutting off my phone as I head to Nate's floor. The receptionist escorts me to his office and asks if I want anything.

"Water would be great." My throat is a desert.

I glance around at his office, a handsome space with a leather couch, a black desk with only a framed photo of what looks to be Nate and his wife, and a manila folder on the wood surface. Pictures of his hotel properties from around the world adorn the walls, as well as another shot of the pretty blond woman with her arms around him under a sunset on the beach. They look happy—100 percent, genuinely happy. I can see it in their eyes.

Nate strides in with a glass of water and hands it to me. "Here you go, Elise," he says with a smile.

I take a gulp and set down the glass, then shake his hand.

"Please take a seat," he says, and nerves scale my body again as I sit.

He leans against the desk. "I met with a few agencies, and it came down to you and Thompson Group."

My shoulders tense. Then, a horrid idea smashes into me. Should I have met with John Thompson after all? Would that have helped? Did I miss a chance again, even though all my instincts told me to stay the course? But meeting with the competition during the pitch phase isn't wise. It's not how it's done.

"We will be outsourcing some of the media work to his shop," Nate says, and I hold my breath. "He really knows some aspects well. But the bulk of the work is yours, and I'm pleased to offer Durand Media the contract to oversee the advertising campaign for our new European resort rollout."

I float to the sky, a thousand stars twinkling brightly. "I'm so thrilled. I can't wait to start."

"Can you go to New York next week? To meet with some of my executives there?"

"I'd love to."

This feels like more than winning. It feels like I can trust my gut again. That is the ultimate victory.

* * *

I head to the soccer field on a professional cloud nine, ready to root for my husband from the sidelines. I'm going to be the loudest wife there is. *Wife.* I didn't think I'd slap that designation on myself ever again.

But being Christian's wife has been more than fun. It's been exactly what I needed in some unexpected way. Even though it's only been a few weeks, I've learned that the institution of marriage, in and of itself, isn't a farce.

Marriage can be a place for honesty, and openness, and communication. I rewind to the way we tease each other, how we talk frankly about nearly everything. I never had that with Eduardo. He was all wine and roses and romantic escapades. He was a master at seduction and he Casanova'd me.

It all felt so thrilling at the time, but as I reach the field and spot the silhouette of a tall, strapping man whose ring matches mine, I'm keenly aware that this marriage of convenience feels infinitely more real. My heart kicks faster when I see Christian, beats harder.

Something powerful, something hopeful is brewing inside me. Come to think of it, the brewing is done. It feels more like my heart is brimming. Christian Ellison has done so much more for me than my first husband ever did, and I can't wait to share my work news, to throw my arms around him, and to holler his name from the sidelines.

When I reach the field, I furrow my brow. He's talking to a woman, and while that doesn't bother me, something about her feels eerily familiar.

I don't know why. Maybe it's in the way she stands, arms crossed at her chest, jaw tight.

In an instant I know who she is, and I burn. I want to tell that con woman she never deserved Christian's brother. I want to tell her for him, for me, and for anyone who's ever been tricked in that sort of nefarious, underhanded way.

Righteous indignation sparks in me as I stride over and wrap an arm around my husband. Possessively. Letting her know we're together. We're a team.

She stares at Christian. "Can we please talk?"

"What do you need to say that can't be discussed in a boardroom?"

Jandy gestures to me. "Is this the new Mrs. Ellison?"

He smacks his forehead. "Oh, wherever are my manners? Jandy, please let me introduce you to Elise Ellison."

I didn't take his name when we married, but I don't mind that he calls me by it now. In fact, I like the sound of it. I wrap my arm tighter around his shoulder as he turns to me.

"Elise, this is Jandy. The woman who broke my brother's heart."

Jandy sighs heavily, as if it's so exhausting to have to hear such a description. She extends her hand to shake. Her skin is cold. "Lovely to meet you," she says, clearly lying.

"Pleasure to meet you."

Christian stares at her point-blank then taps his watch. "Why are you here? I have a match, and I know you disturbed Erik during lunch, which pisses me right the fuck off. Can't you at least let the man have a sandwich in peace?"

I recoil when I hear what she did, and I jump in instinctively. "That's the least you can do. Let my brother-in-law be."

Jandy ignores me and speaks to Christian again, her voice shaky. "Can we talk? Can we work something out? I really need to help my sister. Surely, you can understand helping a sibling."

"I can also understand when someone is full of shit," he says calmly, and I squeeze his arm, proud of him for giving this woman hell. She deserves hell. "You never said a word about your sister being sick, and all of a sudden you pull this notion out of thin air to prey on Erik's sympathies. Well, I've got none for you. Zero. Zilch. You can't prey on mine. I checked her Facebook page, and she went tubing down a hill yesterday."

"That picture was from earlier in the year," Jandy protests, then seems to shift gears, softening her tone. "Please. Let's work together."

He rubs his ear. "What's that you said? Work something out? How on earth could we work something out?"

"I thought we could strike some sort of deal." She gestures from him to me. "Like you two clearly have."

My jaw drops. "Excuse me?"

"Oh, come now. You've been married a couple of weeks." She turns to Christian. "That's when her picture showed up on your Facebook page. Do you think I'm stupid?"

I laugh then cover my mouth.

Jandy glares at me. "Is something funny?"

I raise my chin. "It's funny that you would ask that because I don't think 'stupid' is the word anyone would use to describe you."

She parks a hand on her waist, her elbow akimbo. "What word would you use?"

Oh, she's walking into this one. "Cold."

Christian raises a hand. "Callow."

"Cruel."

I flash Christian a wicked grin. "Classless."

Jandy holds up a hand, but my husband gets in the last dig. "Cutting."

"I second that. You're totally cutting," I add.

"You don't know me," she says, raising her chin. "You don't understand what I've been through."

Christian shakes his head, sneering. "Enough of the whole daddy talk. I don't know what your issues are, and I don't want to know. But this isn't how you treat someone who treated you like the world. You were everything to my brother. He gave you his heart, and you stomped on it like it was rubbish."

Her jaw is set hard, but her eyes are glossy. She

seems to steel herself though, speaking through tight lips. "You don't know me, and this isn't about me."

Christian holds up his hands. "Oh, it's not about you? Then enlighten me. What is this about?"

"I came here because it's clear this is some kind of sham marriage to trick the shareholders."

Christian arches a brow. "Sham marriage?"

"Do you two really think they won't be able to tell you married her simply to try to keep the company?"

"One, my grandfather's trust outlined precisely how the firm would be handed over. Two, Elise and I are legally married, and three—"

"How dare you suggest you know something about our marriage? You know nothing," I say.

She snaps her gaze to me. "I know you married only a few weeks ago. And prior to that, I'd not heard you so much as existed."

I step closer. "And do you know I met Christian more than a year ago? Do you know he asked me out on our first date last June on a boat tour in his hometown? Do you know we were on the same plane flying home? Do you know he courted me for a year?" I grab my phone, click on my handstand photos, and shove the screen in her face, covering his bottom half with my thumb. "Do you know I have pictures of him from that time because I was so utterly transfixed with him, and I believed fate had brought him into my life?"

Jandy stammers, her eyes welling again. "Umm."

"Exactly. You know nothing." I put my phone away, grab Christian's arm, and plant a possessive kiss on his cheek. One that says he's mine. I do it again. And God, I do it a third time, then I turn back to the woman who had inadvertently pushed me closer to him. "You know nothing because our relationship is private, and it has nothing to do with you that Christian is the most wonderful husband in the world. Before that he was a fantastic fiancé, and before that he was an incredible boyfriend. Even before all that, he pursued me and totally won me over. So yeah. Game over. He's mine, and I'm his, and there's nothing you can suggest to anyone in the whole wide world that'll obviate the truth."

I give her a checkmate look, and she huffs. I don't care about her anymore. I care about the man by my side.

I grab his face in my hands and press a searing kiss to his lips that has nothing fake in it at all.

In fact, as I kiss him, the thought flashes like a neon sign turned on. There's nothing fake between us.

Everything, all of it, from my mind to my heart, is genuine.

When we break the kiss, Christian glances at Jandy and makes a shooing gesture. "Off you go."

She leaves, her tail between her legs.

I turn back to him.

"You were amazing."

"I got the account," I blurt out.

"I knew it. I bloody knew it." He picks me up and spins me around. "So proud of you."

"I couldn't have done it without you."

A game whistle sounds.

"I need to go," he says, setting me down. "But we are going to celebrate the hell out of you winning the account."

"Go, go."

He runs to the field, and I spend the next hour watching the man I feel everything for play a game.

I came into this arrangement believing my walls were fortified. That my lessons learned would serve as armor for my heart.

But this time, I wasn't the one fooled. I fooled myself into thinking I could keep from letting him into my heart. That's where he is.

I've fallen in love with my temporary husband.

As he scores a goal and thrusts his arms in the air in victory, I cheer wildly for him. He looks over, a grin lighting his handsome face as he points to me. It's exhilarating, this moment of connection. My heart somersaults, trying to kick its way free and gallop over to him.

I want that. I want that terribly, and more than I should.

But that's the problem. Love isn't supposed to be part of the terms for us, and it's absolutely not permissible for me.

Love is a terrifying choice. That's why I've built walls. He wasn't supposed to tear them down. I wasn't supposed to let him knock them to rubble with all his kisses, and his tender touches, and his sweet and dirty and thoughtful ways with me.

My shoulders tense and curl inward, and I want to simultaneously run to him and run the other way.

Most of all, I want a new road map, one that'll lead me through this unknown terrain where I'll have to fake my feelings for him for the next few months.

\* \* \*

That night nothing is fake.

There's nothing false about the way he looks at me as I undress. Or how he climbs over me and sinks inside.

There's not a single fictional moment between us as I wrap my arms and legs around him and draw him in deep.

He swivels his hips and moves in languid, lingering strokes that drive me to the edge of pleasure, to the edge of the world.

"God. *This*," he whispers roughly in my ear.

"I know."

We fall into silence again because it's too hard to talk, too hard to give words to all these emotions whipping through me like a storm. But as he sweeps his lips against my neck, down my throat, I shudder. It feels like we're making love. Like we're saying new phrases with our bodies. Talking in a bold new language. One that says *I love this*, and *you're mine*, and *let's not stop, let's never stop*.

Soon, I'm seeing stars and saying his name, and this feels like surrendering to love.

It's terrifying and beautiful at the same time.

The bell above the door chimes as I walk into the air-conditioned sugary paradise. Candy welcomes me, and I need it.

Falling in love is the worst. It's total agony, and as far as I can tell, sugar and wine are the only potential antidotes.

It's too early today to hit the bottle. Ergo, I'm here, three miserable days after the realization that I'm stupid for Christian.

Veronica finishes with a customer, and when the gray-haired lady leaves with her bag of red sugar lips, my friend calls me over. She flinches as she studies my face. "Uh-oh."

"*Uh-oh* what?"

She dips her hand into the candy case and grabs a gummy bear. "I can tell by the furrow in your brow that you need this desperately."

"Wouldn't a furrow in the brow suggest I need Botox instead?"

She shakes her head, her ponytail whipping side to side. "These are infused with champagne."

"By all means, then, give me a bottle's worth of gummy bears." I take the squishy candy and pop it into my mouth. A tiny burst of bubbly spills on my tongue.

"Tell me. What brings you to my office? Want to lie down, put up your feet, and tell me all your woes as I feed you candy?"

"Yes, Dr. Candy Freud. That sounds like exactly what I need." I stare at her from across the display. "Also, is it obvious I'm out of sorts?"

She makes a square near my forehead with her hands. "Like a big neon sign that says 'forlorn.'"

I sigh, wishing that it were easier to fall in love. I wish too that I could serve up the truth without feeling like I'm a traitor to myself. But since the night at the club, since the soccer game, since later that same night at my house, I am guilty of treason.

My heart skipped out sometime after midnight and ran away from me, flinging itself at Christian. Now here I am, popping champagne gummy bears into my mouth.

I don't even like gummy bears. I like cinnamon sticks and clarity. I like walls and safety.

And I like Christian. More than all those other things. I like him more than buying gifts. My shoulders sag. "I might, possibly, just a little bit, have fallen for the man I married," I say in a low confession, waiting for the reprimand.

Veronica squeals and punches the air, up, down, over and over, like it's a new workout routine.

I scoff. "Why are you excited? It's awful. My chest

aches. I feel like I have a stomach bug all the time. And my brain is operating at hazy levels, like the weather report inside my head says *smog for miles.*"

She smiles wickedly. "Because I was right. Being right is such a wonderful moment that it must be celebrated."

"Fine, you were right. I'm not a cinnamon stick," I grumble.

She points at me, so pleased with herself, as she speaks in a sing-song voice. "You're a lemon gumdrop, Elise."

I shove another champagne bear in my mouth. "I'm going to turn into a drunk gummy bear."

She rubs her hands together. "What are you going to do?"

"Keep faking it?" I offer.

"Why?"

"Because that's what this is. Now I have to fake things in a whole new way. I have to pretend I don't want to throw myself at him and wrap my arms around him every time I see him. I have to act like I don't want to smother him in kisses and tell him he's the one." I cringe at the words tumbling from my lips. "What's wrong with me? Falling in love is awful. It turns your brain to mush."

She grabs a large silver bowl and stirs the sugar mix in it with a wooden spoon. "Or you could say, 'I want to make hot Viking babies with you.'"

"You know he's only half Viking, right?"

She waves her free hand dismissively. "The babies would be one quarter Viking, one quarter Brit, one quarter French, one quarter American, and one hundred percent awesome." She squeals as she stirs. "And you'd be so cute pregnant. An adorable little creature waddling around in your cute glasses and hot skirts."

I shoot her an admonishing stare. "You're not helping."

"Oh, sorry. Did you want me to say 'I told you so' again? Would that help?" She adopts a too-perfect smile.

"No."

Setting down the spoon, she gives me a stern stare, but softens her voice. "Then what do you need? Elise, you married him. You were and are attracted to him. You learned he's brilliant and wonderful, and you have feelings for him. Do you think he reciprocates?"

An image of Christian over me, his crystal-blue eyes gazing into mine, blasts before me. An involuntary fleet of tingles spreads down my body. Then, as I think about how he talks to me, how he treats me, my heart turns warm, like it's radiating in my chest. "Just because he makes me feel all soft inside, and just because he likes to spend time with me, doesn't mean there's anything deeper."

"Or does it? Maybe it means you can date your husband."

I furrow my brow. "Date my husband?"

"Yes. Date him. Keep going. Screw the expiration date. Just keep on keeping on with him even when the deal expires."

I suppose that's a possibility. We could always finish the job, so to speak, but keep working overtime. Of course, that assumes he wants to, and I've no idea if he does.

My phone rings, and I grab it from my purse. Nate called earlier, asking me to move my flight up to tomorrow, so I did. Maybe it's him again. But I don't recognize the number. In case it's a prospective new client, I answer quickly. "Hello, this is Elise."

"Elise, this is Diana. I'm in town, and I have something that I believe is yours."

The other wife's voice shoots me to another time, as my past shoves itself into my present.

# 32

# CHRISTIAN

"And that's why there are so many sundials in Paris. Thank you for joining me today."

Griffin says farewell to the tour group he's led around the city, showing them some of the curiosities of Paris, from the oldest clock in France to a handful of sundials.

I sneaked onto the tail end. As the crowd disperses, I thrust a hand in the air. "But can you show me another one, please?"

Griffin huffs and gives me an annoyed look. "Did you come here to heckle me?"

"Always. You need hecklers. It makes me happy."

"You need a job."

"I have a job. I'm busy constantly," I say, since tomorrow I'm working for a Danish investor who's in Paris to meet with some potential French business partners.

"Yet, you found time to heckle me. Or did you come

to ask me for advice?" he asks as we walk toward the river.

"Impressive how you'd assume I need your advice rather than your company for a drink, you wanker. We're supposed to be getting a beer."

He laughs. "I never forget beer."

But as we head to the pub, I soldier myself for the true reason I wanted to meet for a pint. "What would you say if I told you that you were right about mixing business with pleasure?"

He laughs as we turn the corner. "Of course I'm right. I'm an excellent judge of everything."

"So, this woman I'm married to . . ."

"Wait, wait. Don't tell me. Let me guess." He stops in his tracks, flings his hand over his forehead, and closes his eyes. "You fell for her."

When he opens them, I shake my head. "Thanks for taking my punchline, tosser. Want to remind me that you warned me about this?"

"If memory serves, you said, and I quote, 'We aren't mixing business with pleasure. We're uniting for two mutual goals.'"

"That sounds like something I'd say."

Griffin claps me on the back. "I like keeping you around because you're so incredibly entertaining. But listen, you're not going to crush her heart, are you?"

"No. Remember when I said she'd break mine?"

He stops once more. His voice drops lower, etched with concern. "Yeah? Has she?"

"Seems destined to happen. She doesn't want anything serious. She's made that clear."

He frowns. "She has?"

"Crystal clear from the start."

"And you do? Want something more?"

I nod. "I want so much more."

"Then I clearly owe you a pint because that's a sad story."

We walk in silence for a bit till we reach our favorite pub. As he pulls open the door, Griffin says, "On the other hand, you could lay it out there for her."

I knit my brow.

He grabs at his chest as if reaching inside. "Take your heart and serve it up on a platter—and hope to hell she doesn't chop it into mincemeat."

I laugh, but it's a sullen sound. Knowing Elise, that'd send her scurrying over her fortified walls into a whole new kind of retreat.

But as Griffin heads inside, I stop at the door, thinking of the other night, the things we said.

What if she feels the same? What if she's starting to figure out that this marriage of convenience has turned, unexpectedly, into something more?

I need to give her time. I need to give her the chance to figure out what I've already learned: we could be more than a deal.

That's what I need to do for the rest of the arrangement. Treat her like a queen and listen for any sign that she might be on the same page as I am.

Then, seize the chance.

* * *

Later that evening, I'm working late at my home. Erik

and I have finished a new deal, and it's coming together beautifully. But it requires a fine attention to detail, and I'm this close to exhausted from reading contracts most of the day.

Erik jumps up from the table where we're working. He paces the living room, muttering.

I glance up from the screen on his fifth lap across the carpet. "You okay?"

"I can't believe she tracked you down at the game the other day," he says, disgust thick in his voice. I'd told him what happened at the match. "I can't believe she's inserting herself into everything."

"Don't let it get to you," I say gently, as I tap the screen. "Let's try to finish this off."

He shoves his hands into his hair. "I can't focus. The more I think about it, the angrier I get. I'm so bloody ticked off."

His jaw is tight, and his eyes are fiery. It's a look I hardly ever see on my brother. "Erik, come on. Let's focus on this, order some takeaway, and watch a stupid show."

He shakes his head vigorously. "I can't. I need to go for a run." He darts into the guest room where he's been staying and emerges a minute later with running shorts and trainers on. He heads to the door in a flurry. "I'll work when I come back. I need to clear my head. See Elise, or whatever you want to do."

He leaves, and I hunker down, finishing the read-through. When I'm done, I decide seeing Elise sounds brilliant, especially since she's leaving for New York soon.

I text her, but she writes back and tells me she's

busy tonight.

Somehow, this bothers me more than it should.

# 33

# ELISE

What does one wear to have a drink with her former sister-wife?

That's a question you won't find in most etiquette guides.

As I peruse my closet, I opt for a skirt and a sleeveless top. It's July, and it's hot in this city.

I stare at my reflection. Should I wear my hair up or down? What's the proper hairstyle for having drinks with the woman who shared the same man with you, unbeknownst to each other?

But it doesn't matter how I wear my hair. Tonight isn't about the odd connection we share. Tonight isn't about him.

It's about what she found of mine, and I can't wait.

\* \* \*

I'm laughing so hard I'm crying.

"Oh God, stop. You have to stop," I say between breaths at the café. "I can't take it anymore."

My one-time sister-wife runs a hand through her thick brown hair as she tells me a story about a book she just acquired at the publishing house she oversees in Barcelona. It's a collection of essays about men who love cats. It's absurd and the sheer absurdity is cracking us up. "And the best thing about men who love cats is they have learned to respect your moods. What could be better training for moods than a feline?"

I chuckle as I lift my glass of red, returning to the last time I had drinks with her. It was like discovering I had a long-lost twin. We'd compared notes about all the strange things we'd had in common our whole lives. Now, we're talking about cats, and work, and life. Diana feels like she could be a friend, if she lived in town. "So, how are you doing? Are you well?"

A smile spreads on her face as she takes a drink of iced tea. "Yes, and I'm getting married again."

My jaw drops. "Seriously?"

She pats her belly. "The reason I ordered no wine tonight? I'm three months pregnant."

I reach across the tiny table and give her a hug. "Congratulations! I'm so happy for you. What's he like?"

With a wry smile, Diana lifts a brow and whispers sardonically, "He's honest."

We both crack up.

"He also likes cats, but not so much he'd write an essay about them."

"That's excellent. That's all you really need."

She raises her index finger. "Honesty, chemistry,

and a loyalty to felines that's in line with my own. We have all those in spades."

"I'll drink double for both of us, then."

"What about you? Have you met anyone? I see you have a ring," she says, as if it's a secret I'm waiting to spill.

And it kind of is.

I stare at my wedding band, and on the surface, the story is too crazy to tell. But those details aren't what matter most. It's what's behind them. "I met someone, and he's wonderful. He makes me happy in a way I didn't think I could be happy again. But sometimes I'm scared to fully surrender to the way I feel for him," I admit, taking a deep breath. "How did you let go of the fear?"

She brings her hands together and imitates diving. "You jump off the cliff."

"That's it?" I ask. She makes it sound so simple.

"You let go of it by letting go of it. It's hard, and it's easy at the same time." She dips her hand into her purse. "And here is this little item. I'm glad it's returning to its rightful owner."

I rub my palms eagerly. I never thought it would find its way to me again. I still won't believe it till I verify it with my own two eyes. "Yes, come to mama."

Diana laughs. "I was sorting through my old boxes, and I came across it in one of his jackets. I remembered you had worn one that was similar last time I saw you, and that's why I reached out. I thought you might want it."

She opens her palm, and I gasp. My heart cartwheels as I reach for the cheap, faux-silver chain with a taxicab charm on it. "I can't believe you found it." I stare at the necklace in wonder. It means nothing, and it means everything. It's just a thing, but it's a thing that's come home. "My brother gave this to me years ago. I had it for most of my life, and I never knew what happened to it."

Diana shrugs happily. "Maybe fate wanted you to have it again."

There's that word again. *Fate.* Does fate have anything to do with the whereabouts of a necklace my brother gave me when I was six? Does fate have any role in anything?

When I put it on, I don't think of my brother. I think of Christian, and I want to tell him that maybe I do believe in fate. Just a little bit. Maybe I do believe we were meant to meet again. Maybe this necklace was meant to come back to me. Maybe everything in my life has led me to this moment. To the realization that all I have to do to find happiness is step off the cliff.

When we're done and it's time to say goodbye, I hug her tightly. "I'm glad you found this, and I'm thrilled to have it again." I tug her closer. "Good luck, Diana. I want you to have a beautiful life."

"I want the same for you."

A lump rises in my throat. I never thought I'd be here today, on the other side. The side of letting go, of being free. But as I walk away, touching my taxicab charm, I'm sure that's exactly where I am.

I'm heading to New York tomorrow, and tonight I want to see Christian. I call him.

"Hello?"

I flinch at the voice on the other end of the line. "Erik?"

"Sorry, yeah. I answered his phone. I just returned home from a long run and he's sound asleep."

"Oh," I say, my heart plunging into disappointment. "He must have been tired."

"He's zonked. How are you?"

I cross the street, doing my best to table my desire to see Christian. "I'm good. And you?"

"Brilliant. Never been better. In fact, I was going to call you."

"You were?"

"I need your help with something, and I know you're already helping with so much already, but I hope you won't mind."

He tells me what he needs. I like Erik. I care about him. I also want to do right for the brother of the man I love.

I say yes, and he tells me he'll swing by early in the morning to pick me up.

# 34

# ELISE

Erik picks me up in an Uber at seven on the dot. I send Christian a text letting him know I'm helping his brother with a project. But I don't hear back from him. "Where's Christian?"

"Griffin convinced him to run six miles or something this morning. He's insane."

"Totally mad," I tease, but a seed of worry gnaws at me. "Is he okay?" It's odd that I didn't talk to him last night, but then again, he went to bed early. Maybe I'm reading something into nothing.

"He's busy at work," Erik says absently, staring out the car window. His mind is clearly elsewhere, and I don't know where that elsewhere is. Erik didn't tell me much. He simply said he wanted a woman's company to pay a visit to Jandy.

"Do you think she's going to listen to me? She didn't seem too fond when she showed up at the match."

He turns back to me. "I'll do the talking. I want you there because she has issues with men, due to a poor relationship with her father. I'm now the man on the outside, so I don't want to set off those subconscious issues."

"I understand," I say, though I don't entirely. But I'm impressed Erik has such a strong read on the woman's psyche.

"I called her sister last night after I finished my run."

I arch a brow, curious. "What did she say?"

His jaw is set hard in anger. "Jandy's story about Lillian being ill sounded dodgy, and I was right on that count. Lillian said she was in a car accident and took a few days off work. She had whiplash. She's not having hundreds of thousands of euros in medical treatment, like Jandy made it seem."

"That's good. It's good she's not ill."

"It also means Jandy is off her trolley."

"Well, yes," I say softly.

When we arrive at the café, Erik thanks the driver, and we snag a table inside. A minute later, the woman who confronted me at the soccer field arrives, stopping in her tracks when she sees me. She points. "What's she doing here?"

"It's easier for me this way, and I think you'll want to hear what I have to say," Erik replies.

"Hello, Jandy," I say, doing my best to be civil, though I'm sure she wants to throttle me as much as I want to throttle her.

"Hello," she says, but her voice is wobbly, and her eyes look tired, as if she hasn't slept in days.

Erik stands and pulls out a chair. Jandy pauses, regards it, then sits.

Erik takes a deep breath and looks straight at her. "I get that you're not in love with me. I truly get it. It hurts like hell, but I'm not going to dwell."

My heart aches for him, and I want to tell him it gets better. Instead, I simply listen.

Jandy murmurs a *thank you*.

Because listening to her husband talk about his feelings would be oh-so-hard. I resist the urge to slap her—mostly because I've never slapped anyone. I'm sure I'd botch it.

"But I need this to stop." Erik's tone is crisp and clear. Dominant, even.

Jandy flinches. "What do you need to stop?"

He slices a hand through the air. "All of it. You coming up to me at lunch, you seeing my family at matches, you making up stories about your sister. It has to stop."

Jandy breathes out hard through her nose. Her top lip quivers. "And you think coming here will make it stop?"

She sounds as if she's trying to be tough, but her will is breaking.

"I have an offer for you."

That makes me sit up taller. He didn't mention an offer.

Jandy shakes her head, worrying her lip, glancing at me. She lowers her voice. "I don't want to discuss this with other people present."

"Please," Erik implores.

She shakes her head and folds her arms.

"I'll step outside," I suggest, since outside is a mere ten feet away.

"That's fine," Erik says.

I leave and pace on the sidewalk, hoping to hell and heaven and back that he isn't caving and giving her his share of the company. I text Christian again to see what he's up to, but he doesn't respond. I spend a few minutes making sure I'm checked into my flight in a couple hours, then I send a note to my brother, since I'll see him soon.

Briefly, I contemplate inviting Christian to join me in New York, and the idea sends a thrill through me. I'd love to show him my old stomping grounds. I'd love to take him around the city, to kiss him in Central Park, along Fifth Avenue, and by the Met.

But I resist. He's clearly busy, and I have work to focus on with Nate and the Luxe. The cliff will have to wait.

Soon enough, Erik steps through the doorway of the café and onto the sidewalk, a gleam of triumph in his eyes.

He doesn't look back at Jandy as she walks along the street, her head tucked down, until she fades into the early morning crowds. He simply walks toward me, a few sheets of paper in his hand.

"You look pleased," I remark.

He beams. "I am. I struck a deal, and she said yes. Let me go track down Christian so we can tell him everything."

I'm dying to know everything too.

* * *

Twenty minutes later, we walk into another café across

the city, and Christian is waiting, drinking a coffee at an outdoor table. He runs a hand through his hair, slick with sweat from his run. A smile seems to tug at the corner of his lips when he spots me, but then it fades. He stands and drops a kiss to my cheek, and I wrap an arm around him, craving a bit of closeness. "Hi." His voice sounds strained.

"Hi," I say, and nerves thread through me. Christian seems cooler than usual. I want to ask him why, but Erik has a bulldog puppy inhabiting him today.

Erik clamps one hand on my shoulder and the other on Christian's, separating us as he chuckles like Santa Claus. "And that kind of show won't be necessary any longer." Erik grabs a chair and parks his hands behind his head, clearly pleased with himself.

"What do you mean?" Christian asks as he takes a seat too. I do the same.

Erik's grin stretches from Paris to Copenhagen. "She sold me her shares."

My eyes widen.

Christian's jaw comes unhinged. "What?"

He slaps the papers on the table victoriously. "I was tired of her games. So I made her an offer she couldn't refuse. I knew when she tracked you down at the match that she was at the end of her rope, so I figured I had a shot at putting an end to this whole ruse." He gestures from Christian to me, and his smile grows. He is the portrait of a proud man. A man who solved a problem. "The two of you were tremendous. You came through for me, and I can't thank you both enough. But I'm tired of being the pathetic loser who begged his brother to marry a woman he was merely shagging so I could stay in charge of a company."

I bristle at the way Erik describes me, especially since Christian and I weren't even sleeping together till after we tied the knot. "Is that how you described this?" I ask my husband.

He slashes a hand through the air. "No. Absolutely not."

Erik waves a hand. He's undeterred. "You know what I'm getting at. The two of you had a deal. You made a deal for me, and I bloody love you for it. But we all know the score. You like each other. But no one is in love here, so you shouldn't have to fake it, and now you don't." He leans back and swipes one palm across the other. "Problem solved."

"What?" Christian and I speak the one-word question at the same time, looking at each other, then at Erik.

I straighten my spine, part my lips, and am this close to asking Christian what his brother means with the whole *not in love* comment, when realization smacks me hard. Erik knows Christian doesn't love me. Of course he knows. They're brothers, they're besties— they know all the things.

My heart crashes to the floor and shatters into thousands of jagged bits. A tear slaloms down my cheek, and I wipe the traitorous evidence away as quickly as I can. Neither one of them notices since they're focused on each other.

My fingers shake, and I hurt.

I hurt everywhere.

"Why did you do this?" Christian asks his brother in a heavy tone.

Erik slams his fist on the table in excitement. "I needed to be a man and solve my shit. So I made her a ridiculous offer for her shares, and she said yes. I figured she's realized her gambit failed, and I bought out her shares for more than they're worth to get her off my back and out of my life. She signed the papers my lawyers drew up, and I'm the majority shareholder again." He beams again, no clue that his news has cracked me in two. "I now pronounce you ex-husband and ex-wife. Why don't you let me buy you breakfast, so Elise can be on her way to the airport?"

I sit in stunned silence, unsure what to say to anyone but the waiter. I ask for a coffee, but when I'm halfway through, I can't take it any longer. I can't take sitting here across from Christian while Erik prattles on about next steps for the firm and deals he wants to put together. He fires ideas at Christian, who weighs in matter-of-factly, as if he's ended one business deal and is embarking on another.

Why on earth should I stay? I'm not needed. This is business for them. We don't need to play pretend anymore.

I stand. "I need to go." I do my best to erase the sound of tears from my voice, but I'm not sure I'm successful. "Flight to catch."

"Your trip is today?" Christian asks, curiously.

I nod as I step away from the table so I can hail a taxi. Erik and I say goodbye, then I answer Christian. "Yes, Nate moved it up by two days. I called last night to tell you, but Erik answered."

"And invited you to go along to see Jandy?" he says, as if he's putting puzzle pieces together.

I nod, swallowing in the words, because if I speak I will break down.

Christian signals to his brother that he'll be right back, then he follows me down the sidewalk, his brow furrowed. "Did you know he was going to make the offer?"

I shake my head, forcing myself to speak as evenly as I can. "No idea. He said he couldn't face her alone."

"He went in there on his own and did it?"

I take a breath. "He said he needed company, and I said yes because I wanted to be helpful."

He nods a few times and hums. "You've always wanted to be helpful."

"I suppose."

He says *okay*, and I can't read his expression or tell what he means. Then he speaks quietly. "He thinks we want to be over."

My heart jams its way to my throat, as a cruel, fresh new realization sets in. Maybe *this* is fate. Maybe fate is trying to save me from jumping off the cliff. "We can be free now, I guess."

"Is that what you want?" he asks, his voice sounding heavier than usual.

Tears sting the back of my eyes as a taxi down the block turns on its indicator light, signaling that it's coming my way. "I want to be happy."

I thought that was with him, but his happiness isn't with me. It's better I know that now, so I can keep moving forward. Absently, I run a finger over the taxicab charm necklace.

"You found it?"

"Diana, the other wife. She was in town. She brought it to me."

He knits his brow. "That's who you were seeing last night?"

"Yes."

He shakes his head and drags a hand through his hair. "You didn't tell me you were seeing her."

"I planned to. I didn't have a chance yet."

"Listen." His voice is heavy. "There's a lot we need to talk about."

I nod as the green car wedges itself along the curb next to me. "I'm sure we'll have paperwork to file."

He grabs my arm. "I'm not talking about paperwork. I'm talking about us."

The cab driver honks, and that's my cue. "Of course." We need to define the terms of the untangling just as we did the entanglement. "I should probably focus on my new account, though, when I'm gone. How about we work out all that stuff when I return?" I paste on a cheery grin as I grab the door handle.

He grabs it too, reaching for my hand. "Let me ride with you. Let's talk now. I can't let you go on this trip with this hanging between us. Even if we don't need to be married, I still want you in my life."

Wanting me in his life isn't the same. It's not the same as what I want.

I want him. I want him as my husband, my Friday-night lover, and my business partner, all rolled in one.

And since I can't have that, I don't know if I can handle anything at all, even if the thought tears me in two.

I bite the inside of my lip. I can't break down now. I can't, and I won't. "I can't talk right now," I say, pushing out the words so I don't let loose a rainstorm.

The driver honks his horn again.

Christian lets go of the handle. "I'll miss you."

"I'll miss you too," I mutter, but I know we mean it in different ways. He'll miss the sex, and I'll miss the everything.

When I get in the cab, slam the door, and reach a respectable distance from him, the tears flow freely. Hard, heavy tears.

This isn't how our part-time love affair was supposed to end.

# 35

# CHRISTIAN

Terms.

Deals.

Financing.

I spend the day enmeshed in them, working in the air-conditioned conference room at a bank. Translating money words all day long is literally the only thing that keeps me from thinking non-stop about everything that went wrong this morning.

There's no space to think about yourself when you're translating, and maybe fate was looking out for me, giving me this assignment on a day when I desperately need to keep my gray matter occupied so I don't dwell on the complete U-turn my life took at a café this morning.

But once the day ends, and the client arrives at a tentative deal, thanking me for helping him converse, I'm free to go.

And my thoughts free-fall the second I leave the

office building, the heat of the late afternoon slamming into me cruelly.

I drop my shades over my eyes, unknot my tie, and walk down the avenue. I weave through the throngs of businessmen and women in their suits and heels, chattering on their mobiles, dragging on their cigarettes.

I shove a hand through my hair and walk.

A few blocks later, I glance at the street sign on the building across the way.

I didn't mean to head in this direction.

I meant to head . . .

Hell, I don't know where I am or where I planned on going.

I don't have a sodding clue.

I thought I'd be seeing Elise tonight.

I thought I'd be working with Erik today.

But I'm doing none of those things, since Erik doesn't need me, and neither does Elise.

I'm back to bouncing between random gigs, filling the time, keeping busy. I like keeping busy, but I don't enjoy feeling aimless. I head to the river and slump down on a green-slatted bench.

All I need is a bag of bread chunks to feed the pigeons, and I'd be a right pathetic sight. Come to think of it, why should the fucking pigeons suffer?

I pop into a nearby boulangerie, grab a baguette, and rip off chunks for the birds.

Some lady tuts at me, shaking her head, and muttering something about not feeding the pigeons.

I don't care.

I toss chunk after chunk at the birds, and let me tell you, they *love* me. They think I'm the bee's knees.

One of them hops up on the bench. "You're a bold little bastard."

He stabs his beak against the bag.

"Demanding, aren't you?"

I grab another chunk and chuck it across the pavement. He flies off and returns a second later.

I make my way through the bread as I stare at the boats cruising along the river and cyclists whizzing by on the path.

When it comes to signals from Elise, the signs seemed bright and clear today. Now that I'm finally away from the bankers, I review them, talking to the daring pigeon, who waits determinedly at my feet.

"First, she didn't mention she was seeing the other wife last night. That's kind of a sign, right? That maybe she doesn't want to tell me things that matter."

The pigeon stares at me.

"Then she said we were free to end things. She wants to be happy. Ending this makes her happy. Obviously, right?"

The pigeon doesn't answer.

"And to top it off, Elise has made her intentions apparent from day one." I heave a sigh. It's stupid for me to linger on why we ended. We were only ever an arrangement.

I stand, brush my hand over my trousers, and toss the final chunk of bread to the pigeon. He wolfs it down then flies away.

Figures.

He got what he wanted.

I walk in the other direction, away from the fading sun, but as I meander, a clucking sound echoes nearby.

I glance up at the branches of a tree. It's the pigeon. At least, I think it's the same one. He's following me.

"I don't have any more. I told you," I tell him.

He's undeterred. He flaps behind me as I walk, stopping in branches along the way.

"It's a lost cause, mate," I mutter.

But it's not lost to him, because he's stuck to me, it seems.

He's persistent.

And as I keep going, and he does too, my brain starts to clear, like clouds are parting. My mind moves aside the terms and the words that demanded all its real estate today. It makes way for new ideas to take root.

Ideas about persistence.

Determination.

Because I can't shake the thought that I was wrong in my conversation with Mr. Pigeon.

Maybe that's just hope talking.

Maybe that's simply a fool's wish.

Or maybe it's determination to see this all the way through.

I call Erik and tell him he needs to meet me straightaway. I've helped him sort out his mess for the last few months. Time for him to help sort out mine.

In the meantime, I send Elise a message.

# 36

# ELISE

On the way to a late lunch with my brother, I reread the texts Christian and I sent this afternoon, trying to find any hidden meaning in them.

**Christian:** Hi. How was your flight? Is Manhattan everything you wanted it to be?

*No. You're not here*, I wanted to shout.

**Elise:** It's fabulous! Always good to be home.

*Nothing is fabulous when you have to fake your emotions.*

**Christian:** Great! Glad to hear. When do you return? Can I take you out to dinner when you're back?

*Why? Why? Why? To tell me you want to keep fucking me every Friday night? That you vastly preferred things when we were part-time lovers only, and why not return to those glory days?*

**Elise:** Sure. Dinner sounds great. I'll be back on Friday.

*Friday. Why do I have to return on a Friday?*

**Christian:** Can I see you then?

**Elise:** Or Saturday. I might be exhausted when I return.

*And I don't want to look overeager.*

**Christian:** Fine, but if you find yourself un-exhausted, let me know. I'd love to see you.

*My pants. You'd love to see my pants.*

I shove my phone to the bottom of my purse as the cabby swerves to The Lucky Spot in Midtown. It's a popular bar, my brother told me, and it recently began serving lunch.

I pay the driver and head inside, grateful I already dropped my bags at my hotel.

My bespectacled brother, Jay, waits at a table, and as soon as he sees me, he stands and waves. My heart lights up with relief. *Family.* I need family right now.

I rush over to him and throw my arms around his shoulders, clasping tight. "So good to see you."

"Well, I didn't expect this kind of greeting."

I don't let go. I hug him tighter, my chin on his shoulder. It's only when I realize his shirt is wet where my cheek rests that it occurs to me I'm crying.

"Elise," he says softly. "What's wrong?"

I separate from him, inhale deeply, and fix on a cheery grin. I wave a hand in front of my face. "Oh, nothing. Long flight. How are you?"

We take our seats, and he narrows his brown eyes. He tilts his head to the side. "You're crying over a long flight? It's eight hours, and you only ever fly first class."

"Not true," I say, straightening my shoulders. "I flew coach to Copenhagen."

My tears crawl up my throat once more. But I catch them before they spill and shove them back down.

"What is going on?"

I tell him everything. "And then I fell in love with

him," I say, plastering on a fake grin. "Wasn't that a fantastic idea?"

He laughs lightly and pats my hand. "It's not as if falling in love is the worst idea in the world."

"Ugh. It is. Love is euphoria and misery cooked into a stew. It's the worst thing ever invented."

He arches a brow over his glasses. "Is it?"

The waiter arrives and asks if we've had a chance to look at the menu. Jay shakes his head, but when I say I'll have a house salad, he opts for a chicken sandwich.

Once the man leaves, Jay peers at my neck. "You found it."

I touch the necklace. "I'm so glad to have it back. It's my little piece of New York."

"You can take the girl out of New York, but you can't take New York out of the girl."

"Do I seem very New York to you?"

"You're tough as nails, so I'd say yes."

"Oh, please. I've cried more times in the last twelve hours than I have in a year."

He smirks. "That's my point. You're so tough, so strong. You're working so hard to protect yourself from getting hurt again. But what if this guy wound up in the same boat as you?"

"What do you mean?"

Jay leans forward, a conspiratorial tone to his voice. "I mean that, at face value, everything you said to him and he said to you leads reasonably to the conclusions you've drawn. But do people really say what they mean?"

"Are you saying he meant something else?"

"If you didn't spell out your feelings, why would you assume he had?"

"Because his brother—"

Jay smiles and wiggles his eyebrows. "Bingo. His *brother* said something. Not Christian."

"But his brother has to know how he feels!"

"I didn't know everything till you told me."

"You live across an ocean. They live together. Erik has been staying with Christian since his wife left him."

Jay shrugs. "Doesn't mean Christian told him how he felt."

I stare at him and speak plainly. "Nor did he tell me, for that matter."

He laughs. "You're making my point exactly."

"And what's that?"

"You're so tough, and you're doing everything to erect skyscrapers around you so you don't get blindsided again. Newsflash—it doesn't hurt any less if you have walls. Once someone gets around them, it still hurts if they don't feel the same as you."

I roll my eyes. "That's helpful."

He smiles and reaches for my hand. "You're already in deep." He takes a beat then shrugs happily. "But it also feels pretty damn good when someone you love feels the same."

"I don't think he does."

"Men don't usually want to talk about *us* unless they feel something," he says, sketching air quotes as he tosses Christian's words back at me.

*I'm not talking about paperwork. I'm talking about us.*

My stomach roils, and the prospect of waiting till

Friday or Saturday to find out what he wants to discuss sounds like an eternity.

Jay lets go of my hand. "Enough about boys. I have something for you." He reaches into his pocket and removes a blue velvet bag, then slides it over to me. "Picked it up at a little shop."

I open the bag to find a silver chain with a dangly Eiffel Tower. I laugh and put it on, letting the icon of France sit next to my taxicab. "It's perfect."

And it gives me strength. It reminds me that no matter what happens with Christian, I have my brother an ocean away. Back home in France, I have great friends, a wonderful life, and a fabulous business I've rebuilt.

That's why my heels are touching the New York sidewalk later that afternoon. Because I made it through a dark time. I turned my agency around, and it's thriving again, thanks to new deals with accounts like the Luxe.

Whatever happens with Christian, I'll be fine, walls or no walls.

I've got this.

# 37

# CHRISTIAN

Erik walks a little taller, a little prouder. The sun is sinking in the sky as he reaches the banks of the river, where I stare into the water.

"Do you ever think this river was meant to be here?" I say, turning to Erik. He shields his eyes from the sun with his hand.

"I've never thought in those terms, but I suspect it probably was."

"Maybe it's supposed to be here because people would need to think and contemplate and wonder."

He stands next to me, setting his elbows on the concrete barricade and gazing at the slate-gray ribbon that cuts across the city. "What's on your mind?"

I heave a sigh. "A few things. First, I really enjoyed working with you at the firm."

"You did?"

I nod. "I did. I liked rolling up my sleeves and tackling deals."

He nudges me. "You angling for a job now?"

I laugh. "No. But it reminded me that I like striking deals and doing market analysis, and not to blow my own trumpet, but I'm also quite good at it."

"You're tops at what you do."

"Thanks." I scrub a hand across my chin. "I think I'm going to keep doing it."

He squints in question. "So you do want a job?"

"No. I believe I've just made myself a consultant."

"Ah, so this is what retirement looks like? Working your arse off?"

"I'd hardly say consulting is working my arse off. In fact, I think it's the perfect balance. I don't get too consumed by it, but it gives me the chance to keep my feet wet. I'll do a little translation, and I'll do a little high-level consulting, especially for companies looking to enter new markets."

"I think that sounds brilliant."

"And that brings me to my other point."

He tenses. "What's that?"

It's not his fault that everything with Elise went tits up, but I need him to know the score. "First, I wish you'd have told me before you made your deal with Jandy."

He frowns. "I'm sorry I didn't. I thought you might talk me out of it because of how much money I'd lose by paying her off," he says, a note of guilt in his voice. "And I was determined to go through with it."

"I get it. I do. I still wish you'd have told me, because I wouldn't have tried to talk you out of it. I wish you knew that."

"You wouldn't have?"

I laugh. "Of course I wouldn't have. It's your choice.

I understand why you did it. Why you needed to. It's your heart and your life. And I'm proud of you for finding a way to move on."

He smiles. "Thanks. It's been total shite, but this is the best I've felt in more than a month."

We both stare at the river for a bit, then I turn to him again. "There is one little matter, though, that ticks me off a bit."

"What's that?"

"I really wish you hadn't told Elise I didn't love her."

His eyes bug out. His jaw falls open. "What?"

"Because that's actually the complete opposite of the truth. I'm pretty much madly in love with her, and now she thinks I don't love her, and I have no clue if she might love me back. But seeing as I helped you sort out your love life, it's time for you to help sort out mine."

He frowns. "I'm so sorry my big mouth fucked things up."

"It's okay. I know you meant well."

He shakes his head. "I'm a bit of a clueless jackass sometimes. But I can also be a determined bastard when it comes to fixing my mistakes." Erik smiles. "I like Elise. I like her a lot. Let's get your girl back." He rubs his palms together. "What's the plan?"

Laughing, I say, "I don't know. That's why I rang you. To devise one."

He furrows his brow, but a minute later, he offers a fantastic idea.

# 38

# ELISE

"That was great. Thank you so much for making all this time," Nate says the next day as he walks me to the elevator banks at his offices in Midtown.

"I'm so excited to get started. These meetings were invigorating. We'll have materials to show you within a week."

"Can't wait."

We say goodbye, and I shoot down to the ground floor, delighted the partnership is starting so well. Even when I leave, I hold my chin up high, determined to enjoy my time in New York. Two days of meetings have been exhausting but energizing.

As I walk up Fifth Avenue, I feel the pull of Central Park, but I'm going to heed another call. That of friends. Last night I fired off emails to some of my favorite women in the city, and I'm meeting them at a bar called Speakeasy.

I reach the establishment, push open the door, and find my redheaded friend Nicole waiting for me. She waves me over. "You're back!" she shouts as she pulls me in for a hug.

"Not to stay, but for now."

She punches my arm. "C'mon. New York is way better than Paris. Don't you want to move here?"

I laugh. "And the campaign to have me relocate begins."

"New York is awesome. We need you here."

"Yes, we do."

I turn in the direction of the new voice. It's Abby, a tiny little blonde I adore. I hug her too. "My New York girls."

After we order, I tell them I require chapter and verse on where they're at with their husbands and children.

"My little angel is finally sleeping through the night. Only took eight months and three weeks to reach that glorious milestone," Abby says, then bats her eyelids as if she's falling asleep.

Nicole pats her knee. "Sleep is the new sex, isn't it?"

Abby laughs. "Yes, but am I greedy to want both sleep and sex?"

I raise a glass. "I see no reason you shouldn't have it all."

Nicole weighs in. "My oldest is finally at nursery school, and he's already an incorrigible flirt."

"Well, he is adorably handsome," I say, since her four-year-old son is the cutest creature on earth.

I dip my hand into my purse and grab two pretty pink bags wrapped with ribbon. "If sleep is the new sex, then candy is the new wine."

I give them their gifts from Paris, a mix of Veronica's

favorite sweets from her shop. "But don't share with the kiddos. Those are just for the moms."

Nicole clutches her bag to her chest. "Mine, mine."

It's only when I say goodbye, with hugs that could go on for days if I let them, and promises to return again soon, that I feel that pang again. That ache that reminds me that I still want a little more.

Actually, I want a lot more.

I stroll up Fifth Avenue. Good thing I changed into flats after my meeting. When I turn into the park, my phone rings.

Quickly, I grab it, and answer the call from my brother.

"Hey there," he says.

"Hey to you."

"Do I get to see you again before you leave?"

"Of course," I say with a smile. "I fly back tomorrow, but I'm free tonight. I'm heading to Central Park now."

He laughs. "Let me guess. The Conservatory Garden?"

"However did you know?"

"Perks of being the big brother. You learn all the habits." He clears his throat. "I need to finish something at work, but I can meet you there in an hour and a half. Does that work?"

"It'll take me time to walk there, so that's fine."

When I reach the gardens, it feels like coming home. I breathe in deeply, inhaling the scents of the Japanese lilacs, the purple cornflowers, and the hydrangeas. I grab a spot on a bench by the fountain and savor the sights.

My heart squeezes tighter in my chest. It beats harder. It wishes for someone.

For one person.

Yes, I am happy without him. But I'd be happier *with* him.

* * *

*Stop and Smell the Days blog*

*July 20: Cliff-diving in a field of flowers*

My lovelies . . .

Here I am in Central Park, inhaling the glory of the gardens. Summer is in full bloom, and all my favorite scents envelop me. I devour the royal purples, the gentle pinks, the blazing yellows, and I drink in the smells of the season wafting around me. This is a flower-lover's paradise, and when I'm here, I'm convinced it is heaven for the senses.

For the sights, especially, and the smells.

And for the heart. I've always felt at home here, ever since I was young. When I visited these gardens, I felt as if I belonged to them. I didn't feel that kind of belonging again until I moved elsewhere, to another city around the world.

And I felt it one other time too.

With a person—one particular person. It's only with him that I feel as if my wild heart has come home.

Time to jump off the cliff.

Yours in noses,

A Scentsual Woman

I hit post, and then, with excitement zipping through me, I call Christian so I can tell him to read it. I'm jumpy and restless, but it's not from nerves. It's from possibility. Even if he doesn't reciprocate, even if he doesn't want the same things I do, I have to take this chance.

For me.

I wait for the phone to connect. It rings, and it rings, and it rings.

Like it's getting closer.

Footsteps crunch across the stone path, and I snap my gaze their way and drop the phone.

## CHRISTIAN

Her phone hits the path with a clatter. Her eyes widen, zeroing in on me as I close the distance, bend to pick up her mobile, and hand it back to her.

I smile because I can't not. She's here. Her brother deserves a medal for telling me where to find her, and for keeping her in one place until I could arrive. She takes the phone, drops it in her purse, and blinks. "You're here?"

"I'm here."

"Why?"

I step closer, cup her cheek, and run my thumb along her jaw. "I came here to tell you something."

"What is it?" Her voice is like a feather.

"My brother doesn't have a clue how I feel. Well, now he does, since I set him straight."

She nibbles on her lip. "What did you set him straight about?"

"I do like you. He was right about that," I say, since a part of me can't resist having fun with the woman I love. "But he was wrong about the rest of it." I raise my other hand and hold her face in my palms, taking a moment to gaze into her beautiful brown eyes. They shine with a look that feels so familiar—because it matches my own heart. "I am in love with my wife."

She gasps and shudders at the same time. "I'm in love with my husband."

And this, right here, is why I flew across an ocean. Why I took this chance. Elise sneaked up on me. I thought we were only fun and games when we started, but then, unexpectedly, she took my heart. She can keep it. She's the only one who gets to have it. "Then, I really should kiss my bride."

She laughs and whispers, "Yes. Please. Now."

I kiss her softly, brushing my lips over hers, savoring what feels like a first kiss. Taking my time, I breathe her in. I linger on her mouth. I want to remember this moment, when everything has finally been said. Our kisses, our touches have always felt real, but now we've sealed our kisses with words.

She kisses me back with such desire, such love that it erases any earlier concerns I had about whether this trip would be worth the risk. She is worth it. She is the risk and she is the reward—the reward I want every day of my life.

When we separate, I press my lips to her forehead. "I thought you were going to break my heart."

Laughing, she wraps her arms around my waist and tilts her face to me. "Why would you think that?"

"Maybe because I wanted you so much from the start. You nearly did break me. I thought you wanted it to be over."

"God, no," she whispers, desperately.

"Yeah?"

"I thought you didn't feel the same."

"Because of my brother?"

She shrugs and nods. "Yes."

"He meant well. But he didn't know the truth. The truth is I've been falling in love with you since the day you agreed to marry me. In fact, I'm pretty sure the first time we slept together, I was already making love to you."

She trembles, and a flush crawls up her neck. It's so alluring, and I want to kiss her all over. "When you came back from London . . ."

The memory of that night blazes before me. "The club, you mean?"

She nods. "I knew it then. I felt it then. That night, our connection—it was the most intense thing I've ever felt."

"Me too, and it wasn't just the sex."

She nods and dusts her lips across my jaw. "I know. It was so much more."

"It can be more. It can be more forever, Elise."

She pulls back and gives me a quizzical look, and that's when I finish what I came here to do. I drop down to one knee and take the box from my pocket, flipping open the lid.

She shrieks and clasps both hands to her mouth.

"Will you stay married to me?"

Her answer comes swiftly. "Yes."

She joins me, pushing me to sit as she climbs on my lap, wraps her arms around me, and smothers me in kisses. "I want to be Mrs. Elise Ellison for always."

I laugh as I tug her close, pressing kisses along her neck. "You never took my name, sweetheart."

"I will now."

I pull back to meet her eyes. "You will?"

She nods. "I want to."

"Do you want your ring?"

"Yes, please." She holds out her hand, and I slide a diamond ring next to her wedding band.

She sighs, and it's a beautiful sound. It sounds like happiness. It sounds like everything I never expected from this marriage of convenience that's now like air to me. *Her.*

"I love it, and I love you, and I want you to read my blog," she says.

"You wrote a blog post?"

She nods, grabs her phone, and shows me a post from fifteen minutes ago. As I read it, my smile can't be contained. I point to the screen. "You posted that as I was walking over to you?"

She nods and grins like a fool. "I did."

I give her a look. "Elise, admit it."

"Admit what?"

I point from her to me. "This is fate. We're fate."

She laughs. "Yes. I believe in fate. But mostly I believe in you." She plants a searing kiss to my lips that makes me want to do very dirty things to her.

I grip her hips, lift her off me. "Let's go to your hotel."

We leave the park and hail a taxi.

"By the way, how did you find me?"

"I tracked down your brother's number and asked

him to find out where you were. He seemed quite eager to make sure you'd be here to meet me."

She laughs. "I'm so glad it was you instead of him."

I run a finger over the hollow of her throat, touching her new Eiffel Tower charm. "We need to get you a necklace for the gardens now. You don't have one. Do you need a flower charm?"

She shakes her head and holds up her hand. "I have a diamond instead."

\* \* \*

We waste no time when we reach her room. Clothes come off at record speed, and our bodies become reacquainted with each other. It's only been a few days since I've seen her, but it's been too long since we've touched.

When I climb over her, and she raises her arms to loop them around my neck, I look into her eyes. "I want to make love to my wife."

She doesn't say yes. She doesn't say, "Make love to me." Instead, she says, "Consume me."

And I do. That's how I make love to her. Like there's a fire inside me, and the only way to quench it is to have her. To take her. To bring her to the edge of pleasure again and again.

I lose track of time. I lose track of her orgasms. She twines around me, her skin hot, her eyes glossy. My hands tug on her hair, and my lips crush hers, my teeth nipping at her neck, her earlobe, her jaw. The sounds she makes send me into another realm. My mind is a blurry haze of desire and love and passion.

And at last, after we come together one final time, I pull her close and whisper in her ear, "I love you. I've wanted to say that for so long."

She runs a hand down my chest. "I love you. And I feel like I belong to you, and you belong to me."

"That sounds about right. There's something pretty spectacular about falling in love with your wife."

* * *

A little later, after I rummage through the hotel fridge, I announce that we must go out to eat. "I'm starving, and I can't subsist on peanuts."

We dress and head outside on a summer night in Manhattan. "Show me around New York City, Mrs. Ellison."

She does, and we extend our trip, staying for the weekend, taking in the sights. I meet her brother and his wife and kids, as well as her parents, since they're back in town after a holiday. We get along fantastically. So well, in fact, that I make sure they know that when they're in Paris next month, we want them at our wedding.

## EPILOGUE

*Elise*

Twilight drapes over Montmartre. Strings of flickering lights hang from the iron posts that hug my courtyard.

That's all I have for my wedding decorations, and that's all I want. With the soft light fading above us in the sky, and the curving cobbled street beyond the front yard, this is the ideal setting.

Christian taps a spoon against a champagne glass, and all our guests quiet down. I stand next to him at the top of my steps, my arm around his waist. "Thank you so much for coming today and for joining us as we tie the knot again," he says.

Our friends and family cheer, and the ceremony begins. There is no aisle to walk down, no flower girls tossing petals, no string quartet playing tunes. This is a simple ceremony, but already it's my favorite one.

Because everyone who matters is here. Gathered in

my small front yard, which blooms with August's soft pink and pale-yellow snapdragons, are all the people who matter most to us. Joy holds hands with Griffin, Erik stands next to Veronica, my family is gathered close, and Christian's mom is here as well as his father and his wife. Christian's not close to his dad, but it still feels right that he's present.

The officiant clears his throat and marries us once again. This ceremony is nearly as fast as our first one, but it's better because we can finally say out loud how we feel.

"I promise to love you, cherish you, and adore you for as long as we both shall live," I tell him, and Christian says the same words to me.

"Kiss the bride, finally, will ya?"

Christian laughs at his brother's directive, then says to me, "I'll keep doing that for the rest of my life."

He kisses me under the twilight sky on our street, in front of my home, where we now live together.

I loop my hands around his neck, and I'm still holding a bouquet of flowers, tied together with a slim rope. It's a true hodgepodge, with a few roses, some stargazer lilies, a couple of daisies, and some zinnias. This melting pot of petals is courtesy of my new blog readers, the ones who follow my occasional posts about flowers. They didn't send me a perfume bottle, and I didn't want one. Instead they chose the flowers for my bouquet. Lilies for beauty, daisies for innocence, roses for love, and zinnias for lasting affection. I love that it's completely haphazard and completely meaningful in a whole new way.

Most of all, I love that the promise of the zinnias feels possible as I kiss my husband once more.

* * *

Later that night, we all go out to dinner down the road, where we pretty much take over the five-table bistro, toasting with endless glasses of champagne and wine. At one point, Christian grabs me as I walk by and pulls me into his lap. He wraps his arms around me and nuzzles my neck. "At last. I can finally be a kept man."

I laugh and drop a kiss to the end of his nose. "You know what that means, if you really want to be my trophy husband?"

"What does it mean?"

"It means you have to service my needs, any night, any time I request."

He puffs out his chest. "I believe I do that already."

"And I think you're pretty damn good at it."

Christian is anything but a kept man. He's his own man, carving out the life he wants, picking up the jobs he wants, whether it's talking all day for dignitaries or businessmen, or advising top companies on entering new markets. He makes his own choices, and most of all, he doesn't let it demand all his attention, like he did in his twenties. He's learned how to take in work at a pace that makes him happy.

As for me, I'm still working hard, and hope to for a long time, since I love my job and taking care of my employees. Most of all, I love having the kind of relationship that consumes me at night and brings me peace during the day.

I suppose it was fate that brought Christian into my life one fine summer day on a boat tour, but it's not going to be fate that keeps him in it.

It's going to be me, loving this man, and giving him my heart all the days of my life.

# ANOTHER EPILOGUE

*Elise*

*Four years later*

At last.

I have a moment alone to put up my feet and savor the quiet. The boys are outside in the backyard, and I'm away from the crazy day-to-day life of the agency back in Paris—the agency that Polly has been helping me run, now that I've become a little busier at home.

Busier baking.

Baking people.

I run a hand over my belly. It's the second time it's been this big, and there are a few people who are quite happy about that. Me, of course. My fabulous husband, who's an even better father. And his mother. She is, quite simply, the perfect grandmother, and she's convinced us to spend more time here in Copenhagen, so she can dote on her grandchildren.

I don't mind being here at all. It's no hardship to

spend time at Christian's home on the canal, especially during the glorious late summer days when the water gleams like a sapphire, mirroring the powder-blue canvas above us in the sky.

But right now, I simply need to sit.

I close my eyes, but the second I do, a little voice calls out to me.

"Mummy, come look!"

I sigh but heed the call of my three-year-old son, James. Rising slowly, I head to the sliding glass door and step into the yard.

The sun is glaring, and the reflection is so bright, I can't quite make out what Christian and James are doing. But as I shield my eyes with my hand and squint, it becomes patently obvious.

"I can do handstands just like Daddy."

I groan and march down the yard, shaking my head at my husband. "You're not making him part of that club."

Christian holds up his hands ever-so-innocently in a *who, me?* "Of course not. I'm fully clothed."

"Do it with me, Daddy."

Christian flips over on the dock, onto his hands like our son. At least this time, both are wearing shorts.

I smile and relent. After all, maybe the world needs more men who can do handstands, naked or not.

I run a hand over my belly. "Just don't teach our daughter to join your club."

Christian laughs, flips over, and stands up. He rushes to me and sets a hand on my gigantic basketball. "Good point. No daughter of mine will ever be flashing tourists naked."

"She better not."

"But you can flash me later." He winks, and then James runs over and joins us, and I take his little hand. We walk to the dock, sit on the edge, and watch the boats go by.

Happily.

THE END

## ALSO BY LAUREN BLAKELY

FULL PACKAGE, the #1 New York Times Bestselling
romantic comedy!

BIG ROCK, the hit New York Times Bestselling standalone
romantic comedy!

MISTER O, also a New York Times Bestselling standalone
romantic comedy!

WELL HUNG, a New York Times Bestselling standalone
romantic comedy!

JOY RIDE, a USA Today Bestselling standalone romantic
comedy!

HARD WOOD, a USA Today Bestselling standalone
romantic comedy!

THE SEXY ONE, a New York Times Bestselling bestselling
standalone romance!

THE HOT ONE, a USA Today Bestselling bestselling
standalone romance!

THE KNOCKED UP PLAN, a multi-week USA Today and Amazon Charts Bestselling bestselling standalone romance!

MOST VALUABLE PLAYBOY, a sexy multi-week USA Today Bestselling sports romance, and MOST LIKELY TO SCORE, a sexy football romance!

THE V CARD, a USA Today Bestselling sinfully sexy romantic comedy!

WANDERLUST, a USA Today Bestselling contemporary romance!

The New York Times and USA Today Bestselling Seductive Nights series including *Night After Night*, *After This Night*, and *One More Night*

And the two standalone romance novels in the Joy Delivered Duet, *Nights With Him* and Forbidden Nights, both New York Times and USA Today Bestsellers!

Sweet Sinful Nights, Sinful Desire, Sinful Longing and Sinful Love, the complete New York Times Bestselling high-heat romantic suspense series that spins off from Seductive Nights!

*Playing With Her Heart*, a USA Today bestseller, and a sexy Seductive Nights spin-off standalone! (Davis and Jill's romance)

21 Stolen Kisses, the USA Today Bestselling forbidden new adult romance!

*Caught Up In Us*, a New York Times and USA Today Bestseller! (Kat and Bryan's romance!)

*Pretending He's Mine*, a Barnes & Noble and iBooks Bestseller! (Reeve & Sutton's romance)

*Trophy Husband*, a New York Times and USA Today Bestseller! (Chris & McKenna's romance)

*Far Too Tempting*, the USA Today Bestselling standalone romance! (Matthew and Jane's romance)

*Stars in Their Eyes*, an iBooks bestseller! (William and Jess' romance)

My USA Today bestselling No Regrets series that includes

*The Thrill of It* (Meet Harley and Trey)

and its sequel

*Every Second With You*

My New York Times and USA Today Bestselling Fighting Fire series that includes

*Burn For Me* (Smith and Jamie's romance!)

*Melt for Him* (Megan and Becker's romance!)

and *Consumed by You* (Travis and Cara's romance!)

The Sapphire Affair series...

The Sapphire Affair

The Sapphire Heist

Out of Bounds

A New York Times Bestselling sexy sports romance

The Only One

A second chance love story!

Stud Finder

A sexy, flirty romance!

# ACKNOWLEDGMENTS

Thank you to KP Simmon, Helen Williams, Kelley, Jen, Dena, Kim Bias, Lauren Clarke, Karen, Tiffany, Lynn, Janice, Virginia, Stephanie and Michelle. I am immensely grateful for all you do every day. Big thanks to my family, and as always, I am most grateful for my readers, who make everything possible.

# CONTACT

I love hearing from readers! You can find me on Twitter at LaurenBlakely3, Instagram at LaurenBlakelyBooks, Facebook at LaurenBlakelyBooks, or online at LaurenBlakely.com. You can also email me at laurenblakelybooks@gmail.com

74820682R00170

Made in the USA
Middletown, DE
31 May 2018